The phone in Bolan's hand exuded a chilling malice

It took a moment for Bolan to identify the mocking laughter, and he waited, swallowing his rage. Quietly, he addressed himself to Evil. "Yes?"

"You're dead, hotshot."

Bolan waited.

"Trouble is, you're too damn dumb to know it."

Still Bolan waited. An edge was creeping into the voice, and the soldier knew that he had found a nerve. But he continued to remain silent.

"Goddammit, boy," said the voice. "I'm coming after you."

Then The Executioner chose his words deliberately, before the vulture could continue.

"Don't bring anything you can't afford to lose," he said softly.

D0973764

MACK BOLAN
The Executioner

DON PENDLETON's EXECUTIONER

MACK BOLAN

Prairie Fire

A GOLD EAGLE BOOK FROM

W🌐RLDWIDE

TORONTO · NEW YORK · LONDON · PARIS
AMSTERDAM · STOCKHOLM · HAMBURG
ATHENS · MILAN · TOKYO · SYDNEY

First edition August 1984

ISBN 0-373-61068-8

Special thanks and acknowledgment to
Mike Newton for his contributions to this work.

Copyright © 1984 by Worldwide Library.
Philippine copyright 1984. Australian copyright 1984.

All rights reserved. Except for use in any review, the
reproduction or utilization of this work in whole or in part
in any form by any electronic, mechanical or other means,
now known or hereafter invented, including xerography,
photocopying and recording, or in any information storage
or retrieval system, is forbidden without the permission
of the publisher, Worldwide Library, 225 Duncan Mill Road,
Don Mills, Ontario, Canada M3B 3K9.

All the characters in this book have no existence outside the
imagination of the author and have no relation whatsoever to
anyone bearing the same name or names. They are not even
distantly inspired by any individual known or unknown to the
author, and all the incidents are pure invention.

The Worldwide Library trademarks consisting of the words
GOLD EAGLE and THE EXECUTIONER are registered
in the United States Patent Office and in the Canada Trade
Marks Office. The Gold Eagle design trademark, the Executioner
design trademark, the Mack Bolan design trademark, the globe
design trademark, and the Worldwide design trademark
consisting of the word WORLDWIDE in which the
letter "O" is represented by a depiction of a globe, are
trademarks of Worldwide Library.

Printed in Canada

All the great struggles of history have been won by superior willpower wresting victory in the teeth of odds or upon the narrowest of margins.

—*Winston Churchill*

Maybe I'm the ultimate optimist. I believe my sword hand is guided by thoughts of victory. I command myself to win. Therefore, I have the advantage.

—*Mack Bolan*

To the eighteen U.S. Marines who died tragically during the "Team Spirit '84" military maneuvers. God keep.

PROLOGUE

Death was no stranger to Mack Bolan. The Warrior and the Reaper were old acquaintances, with a grim accommodation reached across the years. Sometimes they worked in concert, other times at odds, no friendship or enmity between them. Death was neutral, first cooperating with the soldier, then conspiring to defeat him, both with fine impartiality. In time, Death would consume him as it had so many others on the hellfire trail.

In time. Perhaps today.

This soldier had no fear of death. A realist, Bolan had resigned himself to the inevitable ending of his Everlasting War, but resignation was a far cry from surrender. In the face of death, he was living large and making every moment count, determined to inflict the fullest measure of destruction on his enemies before the end. While life and strength remained, his war continued.

And the warrior's personal crusade had come full circle. Launched in anger, as a quest for private vengeance, it had grown into a holy war against the Mafia's killer legions. From a limited engagement to a global power struggle, Bolan had applied his expertise at jungle warfare to a rather different wilderness. The urban jungle's denizens had come to know and fear him, elusive and indomitable, as he fought against the odds.

In the end he had achieved a victory regarded by the experts as impossible, but his achievement bore a price.

On a rainy afternoon in Central Park, the soldier had surrendered his identity, to be reborn as Colonel John Macklin Phoenix, human spearhead in another everlasting war.

The enemy was terrorism now; the killground was anywhere fanaticism sought to throttle freedom with bloody hands. Committed to his war and supported by a team of dedicated allies, Bolan took the battle to his enemies on every front, continuing the brushfire struggle of attrition that had begun for him in Vietnam so many lives ago.

Belatedly, with countless provocations on the record, Bolan's land of liberty was going hard, fighting back. And for the first time, in a decade marked by losses and humiliation, she was winning—thanks to Bolan and his Stony Man teams. Cautiously, and then with greater confidence, America began to hope.

Then seemingly from nowhere, polluting everything it touched, a lethal human parasite had undermined the war on terrorism and brought the holocaust to Bolan's Blue Ridge Mountain sanctuary. In a single stroke this faceless adversary had signed the Phoenix death warrant, driving Bolan back into the murky underground without cover, without official sanction.

The Executioner was on his own again, one man against the savages. And once more he had a private score to settle—for the death of April Rose, his lady love, and for all the other damage to his friends. But the stakes transcended any personal vendetta. Compared to Bolan's current foe, the Mafia and urban terrorists diminished into paltry insignificance.

The Soviet KGB had run afoul of Bolan and his warriors several times before its undercover operative engineered the firestorm at Stony Man Farm.

For months before the final strike, there had been indications of a guiding hand behind the random acts of terrorism that had slaughtered hundreds, held a frightened world in thrall. And finally, as the battle smoke was lifting from the shambles of his Virginia haven, Bolan recognized the hand, identified its owner and the sinister design behind its machinations.

He was up against the KGB, damn right, and all the varied rumors had been verified in spades. Of course, the plan had never been for Bolan to confront the global threat alone, but he had learned to play the cards as they were dealt, to bet the limit every time and never fold. He would identify the evil and cauterize its deadly tentacles anywhere they could be found—behind the Iron Curtain, inside war-torn Afghanistan, or in America itself.

Without official cover, Bolan's reentry to the States had been a problem in itself, but one the Executioner had solved before. In another life, the world's most wanted fugitive had mapped the hidden highways of the underground, used them more than once when *mafiosi* had attempted to escape his wrath by traveling abroad.

He knew this shadow world as the postman knows his route, every twist and turn memorized, and he was privy to the messages that traveled there by word of mouth.

The grapevine had alerted him to danger on the

home front, and Bolan had responded with alacrity. He carried the advantage of surprise—and very little else—against his stateside enemies, and it could be enough. If they were careless. If they let their guard down for a fraction of a second.

If.

And he had blown it.

His enemies were getting better at it, learning swiftly from their past mistakes—or perhaps his luck was simply turning. Either way, the Executioner had faced a grim reminder of his own mortality, and he was far from being out of danger.

Quite the opposite, in fact. From all the indicators, he was looking at the worst of it ahead and moving into dead collision with the storm.

But he was not afraid of dying in the cause, of joining April and the others who had gone before him. He could accept the thought of death with equanimity—but he could not surrender.

Compromise with Evil was unthinkable, and he would die as he had lived—with fire and thunder—rather than allow himself to be diverted from his course.

Bolan chose the purifying flames, and he would bear the torch against his enemies relentlessly until the fire consumed them all together. And with that decision made, he took the only path available.

The fire was waiting.

1

It was dry and dusty in the corn. A gentle breeze had risen from the south, rippling the living stalks, but its caress escaped the man who lay facedown between the rows.

He had lain motionless for half an hour, since the final burst of desperate energy ran out, and cursory examination would have passed him off as dead. But small, persistent signs of life remained: the shallow rise and fall of labored breathing; beads of perspiration that collected on his brow and underneath his eyes before they joined to trickle down the dust-caked cheeks; a rusty stain against his ribs that glistened now with fresher, brighter crimson at its center.

He was still alive, but time was running out. Another night outside would finish him.

He had to move or die where he lay.

An eyelid flickered, opened. Glazed eyes focused. Time to move, and damn the pain of battered flesh, exhausted muscles.

The fallen runner struggled up and off his belly, supporting his weight on knees and knuckles, biting off a ragged moan as pain assaulted him in nauseating waves. He waited for the worst of it to pass, aware that it was now or never. He was losing it, and there would be no second chance.

The wound beneath his arm had opened up again, and he could feel the blood oozing against his ribs, already soaking through the fabric of his skinsuit. A bullet crease along his thigh was superficial, crusted over where the slug's passage had released a scarlet stream. Manacles had lacerated the flesh around his wrists, but the runner's hands were numb from lack of circulation. Before he lost the use of them completely, he would have to lose the cuffs, and soon.

Priorities, a tiny voice reminded him from somewhere close at hand. First things first. He had to put some ground behind him, find a temporary haven. Hands would be the least of it if he was overtaken there, exposed, defenseless.

The hunters would be running grids behind him, scouring the countryside and homing on the scent of blood. His spoor was plain enough, and they would have him soon, unless. . . .

A superhuman effort brought the runner staggering to his feet. He kept his balance with the force of willpower alone. Exhaustion and the loss of blood were dragging at him, threatening to pull him down, but grim determination drove him stumbling on. His scuffling passage raised a cloud of Kansas dust between the rows of seed corn.

The wall of silent stalks on either side was taller than his head, obscuring his view beyond the narrow alleyway. Overhead, the sun had passed its zenith, indicating that it was early afternoon and that his dusty runway stretched along an east-west axis.

Southward the Interstate—alive with danger

now—extended like an asphalt scar across the landscape. They would be waiting for him there, expecting him to flag a ride, and so he put the sun behind him, trudging to the east.

He had a chance—a slim one—if he could intersect an access road, pursue it undetected to the nearest farmhouse. Then he could get his hands on tools, perhaps a car. Wheels would give him a slight edge on his pursuers.

Moving doggedly along the irrigation trench, he dismissed the defeatist train of thought. He concentrated on the simple task of walking, his bleary mind trying to grapple with time. It was the second day since his escape and he reckoned he had been averaging a dozen miles a day, avoiding major roads and open country where he could.

The fields of corn and wheat had slowed him down, but they provided necessary cover from his relentless trackers. Once—the previous afternoon—he had discovered a slow-moving stream and slaked his thirst, but he had eaten nothing since breakfast on the morning of his capture.

His hunger was the least of all his problems. He would collapse from loss of blood long before he starved to death. And if he tried to save some time by taking to the roads, he could expect a similar result— the silent death-stroke of a sniper's bullet.

So it would have to be the fields, whatever happened there. At least until he found a better hiding place. Exposure at the moment would be suicidal, and the runner still retained a working sense of self-preservation.

The hours ran together in his fevered mind, hallucination merging with reality to yield an endless waking nightmare. Faces and remembered incidents appeared and vanished until the cornstalks themselves loomed forbiddingly, transformed into lurking enemies. He recognized the warning signals of collapse, but realized that if he stopped to rest, he would never rise again.

If luck had spared his life initially, it would require a special kind of stamina to make the save complete.

At first he thought the house and barn were a mirage, but a second glance assured the runner that his eyes were not deceiving him. His quickening pulse betrayed a new excitement, but he suppressed the rush and struggled into a prone position, peering out between the rows of corn.

Reconnaissance was vital. He could destroy whatever chance he had with one false step.

The farmhouse was a single-story wood frame with a covered porch in front. From where he lay, the runner noticed that wire mesh enclosed the porch, preventing him from checking out the door and windows there. And anyone who cared to glance in his direction had an unobstructed view—or shot—if he advanced across the forty yards of open ground.

He scanned the narrow yard, populated by a dozen chickens, to the barn directly opposite. Double doors at either end were standing open, giving him a clear view of the interior. From where he lay, there was no sign of human life inside.

The runner's mind was ticking off the possibilities. There would be tools inside the barn—an ax or hammer, maybe a hacksaw—anything to rid him of the handcuffs. Something that could double as a weapon. But that would come later. . . .

He decided not to approach the barn directly. Instead, he opted for a blind-side run, restricting his exposure to the final moments of approach and entry. All he had to do was shift another twenty yards to the left and he'd put the barn between himself and anyone inside the house.

He wriggled back along the trench on knees and elbows, until he was sure that no one in the farmhouse could observe his move. Satisfied, the runner worked himself into a kneeling position, using the nearest of the stalks for support as he gained his feet. Fatigue had turned his leg muscles to jelly, scarcely able to bear his weight.

Moving parallel to house and barn, he blundered headlong through the rows of corn. With throbbing hands he battered the stalks aside, felt them snagging at his clothing, drawing blood from arms and face. By the time he reached a vantage point behind the barn, the runner was drained of energy.

And still there was no time for rest.

The barn was beckoning, its cool interior inviting. There lay sanctuary and the opportunity to rest. A few more steps and he could be inside.

The runner broke from cover, his shackled hands impeding the momentum of his progress. His equilibrium thus upset, he almost fell on his face before he found his stride. Thirty yards of open ground, and no one opposed him. Twenty, and his tortured throat and lungs were screaming for oxygen; colored flecks of light were swimming behind his eyes. Another ten and he could feel the soothing shade even before he reached it.

There was a momentary risk before he made the open

double doors, but no one tried to stop him. With a final lurching rush, he gained the haven that he sought, the welcome darkness reaching out to envelop him. He collapsed against a wall to gain his breath and bearings.

As he had surmised, the cavernous interior was empty. Half a dozen paces before him, a wooden ladder offered access to the hayloft, and tools were ranged along the southern wall. From all appearances—the homemade workbench, oily stains upon the floor—his hiding place was more garage than livestock shelter. Guessing, he decided that it housed a pickup truck or tractor.

But the owner could return at any moment and find him loitering. And in his present situation, that discovery could be tantamount to death.

From where he stood, the runner spied a hacksaw on the wall above the workbench. Later, when his unknowing hosts had settled down to sleep, he would have use for it. At the moment, though, concealment was the top priority. Concealment and a chance to rest in peace.

The irony of that did not escape him, and he grimaced, shaking off the deadly lethargy that sought to numb his senses. He would rest in peace, damn right, if he relaxed his guard too much.

He started toward the ladder like a prisoner bound for the gallows. If they found him here, there would be no escape. Against determined enemies with guns, the loft was indefensible, a death trap—but it was all he had.

He became aware of a nagging hunger, his stomach growling on empty.

A rank of nesting boxes, for the chickens he had seen, was built against the nearest wall. Alert to any sound of movement from outside the runner detoured, rummaged briefly through the straw, and came away with three eggs. Without a moment's hesitation, he cracked the shell with his incisors, sucking out the contents.

The famished runner savored every drop and thought that it was enough—almost—to keep his belly quiet for the moment. Later, he would raid the nests again, or venture out with darkness to forage for some other nourishment.

The fugitive spent a moment gathering his meager strength before he tried the ladder. Muscles in his arms and shoulders screamed, his hands like grappling hooks, devoid of feeling on the rugged wood.

The runner concentrated on his leaden feet that felt so ponderous and unsteady on the rungs below. He struggled upward inch by inch until his elbows braced against the floorboards of the loft itself. With a final desperate heave, he put everything he had into the effort, and at last he lay facedown upon the rough boards.

He rolled onto his back, grimacing at the pain in his side. Slowly he sat up and propelled himself with heels and elbows toward the interior of the loft until he came to rest against a bale of hay.

He wriggled his body into his straw bed and could feel exhaustion overtaking him. The runner let himself relax, setting his mind adrift. Sleep was welcome when it came, but it was not without some perils of its own.

And he could not escape the dreams.

2

First, before the pain, Mack Bolan became aware of movement. Padded upholstery with the smell and feel of leather pressed against his cheek. On the seat beside him, another body shifted heavily, the cushions squeaking beneath the weight.

Cautiously, Bolan raised an eyelid. Beyond the tinted glass, fields of the dusty gold and pale green of corn and wheat alternated in a checkerboard effect. In front of him loomed the driver's head and shoulders.

The Caddy crew wagon held a steady pace across the Kansas-flat terrain, its radials devouring the two-lane blacktop. In a flash the Executioner remembered where he was, the images rolling across his memory. For an instant, he was back inside the factory and fighting for his life.

Only hours before, Bolan had learned of a plot by subversive offshore forces to sabotage a facility that supplied the U.S. government with "special" computer chips. The word was that the invaders wanted to get their hands on the plans of a secret manufacturing technique that enabled the plant to produce chips from commonplace material. Then they would blow up the lab.

It was supposed to be a soft probe—reconnaissance and nothing more. But no amount of planning could have anticipated that the infiltrators' sentry would surprise Bolan in the laboratory. No amount of speed or accuracy with his silenced automatic could have prevented the lookout's .38 from discharging and bringing the intruders' army on the run.

And Bolan's soft probe had become a hard withdrawal, one determined man against the odds. He had discovered the proof he sought inside the lab. But evidence was useless if he never got a chance to pass it on.

The enemy had been skilled. Initial scrutiny had not revealed the full extent of their defensive preparations, and the Executioner had found himself surrounded inside the plant. Riflemen had cut him off at every turn and while the soldier reduced the odds, they deprived him of the combat stretch he needed to survive. Another moment and the hostile guns would have had him boxed in completely.

The stun grenade had taken him entirely by surprise—a nearly fatal error—and it had left the warrior with a narrow range of choices. He could move or die and in the circumstances, that boiled down to no alternative at all.

He had moved with all the speed and skill derived from years of living on the edge.

He had almost made it.

The explosion, when it came, had been like a thunderclap. Concussion had lifted him, propelled him forward like a human cannonball in some demented circus act. He had cleared a metal catwalk railing, plummeted fifteen feet and struck the concrete floor below with crushing force. Suddenly deprived of oxygen, he had fought to breathe, to rise, and then the troops were on him, boots and rifle butts descending, drumming him into unconsciousness.

They could have killed him, *should* have killed him then and there. It had been a tactical mistake to let him live, unless. . . .

It clicked for Bolan, and he slowly opened his other eye. But the knowledge made his blood run cold. *Unless they had some use for him alive.*

No time to ponder motives now, and any way it went for him the end result would be the same. Alive and free, he was a deadly liability. When they were finished with him—in an hour, in a week—they would liquidate him instantly.

If he gave them the opportunity.

He started checking out the damage slowly, unobtrusively, attempting to discover how severely he was injured. Bruises everywhere, alive and throbbing with a score of different aches that merged together into one—but they were concentrated on his shoulders and along his spine. He tensed the muscles there, shifting slightly with the motion of the Caddy, careful not to let his captors know he was awake. No pain from broken bones, and he began to flex manacled arms and each leg in turn, found everything in working order. The handcuffs were a problem, granted, but nothing insurmountable.

A gravel voice beside him interrupted the silence of the car's interior. The words were directed to the driver.

"How much longer?"

"Twenty minutes. Thirty, tops."

"Hell."

"Relax. It's easy duty."

"Easy, my ass."

He could have sprung the door latch and plunged headlong onto the pavement, but he dismissed the thought. At this speed, if the fall didn't finish him, the gunners would reverse their track and plow him under long before he could recover.

No, he had to neutralize the hostile guns before he made his break. And if it turned out right he might even end up with wheels.

Bolan made his move, leaning hard into the door and pivoting on one hip, bringing both knees up against his chest with agonizing swiftness, heels together. To his right, the startled gunner was reacting, but he did not have the time for an effective countermove.

Bolan's heels impacted squarely onto target, smearing the hoodlum's nose across his face and taking a flap of cheek along with it. The man's head snapped back from the blow, cracking his skull against the window. Bolan locked his wrists around the unprotected throat, his manacles a tight garrote biting into yielding flesh.

The wheelman brought both hands up, struggling to break the stranglehold, and at once the tank began to drift, weaving back and forth across the center stripe at seventy miles an hour. The Caddy must have been on cruise control because the wheelman's legs were thrashing wildly.

Bolan hauled him backward, up and out of his seat, keeping the relentless pressure on. One of those flailing feet found purchase on the steering wheel and then slid through, twisting it hard to the right as he tried to struggle out of Bolan's death grip.

Responding to the sudden turning of the wheel, the Caddy swerved, screaming into a broadside skid. The steering locked from the weight of the man's leg on the spoke, and the car began to capsize. Everything was upside down and spinning, the landscape blurring in a mad kaleidoscope. Bolan and his captors were thrown together, then apart, like dummies in a highway-safety test.

Somewhere in the tumbling confusion, the driver slithered free—but not before his neck snapped audibly, the limp head twisting right around to glare at Bolan with accusatory eyes.

With a crunching jolt of twisted metal on stone the Caddy came to rest on its side. Battered worse than ever and wedged into a fetal ball, Bolan smelled the pungent fumes of gasoline—and something else. The scorched-rubber smell of smoldering electrical wires.

There was no time to lose.

He scrambled up and shackled hands found the jagged outline of a shattered window. He quickly cleared it, disregarding pain and the sudden bloody slickness of his fingers. Bracing a boot heel against the leather-padded headrest of the driver's seat, Bolan pushed up and out of there, jackknifing across the crumpled door. He kicked free, sprawling onto the gravel, the oily undercarriage of the Caddy only inches from his face.

A thread of smoke curled upward and away, at once supplanted by another, growing swiftly. Bolan struggled up and started to run, awkward and unsteady, weaving like a drunkard but putting precious ground between himself and the time bomb ticking at his back.

A pistol cracked behind him, and the bullet kicked up dust a few yards to his right. Incredibly, the second gunner had regained his senses well enough to find his weapon and open fire on the fleeing man. Another round sizzled through the air inches from Bolan's ear.

Dodging to his left, the runner risked a backward glance and caught a fleeting glimpse of the gunman. He was standing upright in the capsized Cadillac with both arms braced across the door, his bloody face a blur above the automatic pistol.

Bolan tried to veer away—and took the next bullet in his side. It opened fabric and flesh, plowing along the curve of his rib cage in a flash of blinding pain.

He staggered, nearly falling, and another slug traced fire along his thigh before the Caddy's fuel tank detonated into heavy metal thunder, swallowing the gunner's scream and everything in roaring flames.

Bolan wasted no time looking back. He was all the way across the road now, into the field. With a dozen loping strides he left the highway, wheat closing in behind him like a soundproof curtain being drawn together.

And his run became an endless nightmare marathon. He ran against the clock, against the odds.

Death itself was breathing down his neck. At any moment now the fingers, pale and skeletal, would reach for him and close around his heart.

How long would it take for the hunters to find him, overtake him in the fields? He had a lead, the slim advantage of surprise, but it was more than counterbalanced by the vehicles at their disposal. He could dodge them temporarily by hiding in the wheat and corn, but if they brought a chopper into it, began to seek him from the air. . . .

Preoccupied, he lost his footing, stumbled and fell headlong between the rows. At once the soldier's intuition told him he was not alone, that he was being followed through the fields.

A sound, the rustle of a footfall in the grain. It was elusive, and he froze, afraid to rise and give himself away. The enemy was closer than he had imagined possible.

The sound of footsteps was repeated, closer now, and he could almost hear them breathing just beyond the nearest row of silent stalks. Bolan held his breath, aware that any sound would bring them down upon him like a flock of vultures.

There was still a chance, of course. It sounded like a single hunter, probably the pointman for their killer team. If he could silently take out the scout and snatch his weapon. . . .

The hand upon his shoulder startled Bolan. He struggled out of sleep to instant, groggy consciousness. Seizing a slender wrist, he put his weight behind the move, abruptly dragging his assailant to the floor. A knee impacted on his side, igniting flares of pain, but he ignored the sudden agony, boring in desperately to neutralize the hunter's weapon.

And his opposition was surprisingly small, yet sinewy and strong. In his weakened state the soldier had his hands full with the flailing figure beneath him. He would have to strike a telling blow while he had the chance.

His arms were raised, the fingers of his two hands interlaced and ready to deliver a death-blow to the larynx when he hesitated. Something in the high-pitched voice, the supple body, stayed his hand. The warrior realized at once that his assailant was un-armed; in a heartbeat he experienced the second jar-ring revelation.

His attacker was a woman.

3

The Cowboy lit a thin cheroot and filled the Lincoln with its pungent smoke. He chose the rank cigars deliberately—as he had the Stetson, mirrored aviator's glasses and the hand-tooled boots—to cultivate an image.

The image was important to his business. It set him apart, made the Cowboy stand out in a field of drab competitors. And the Cowboy got results. In a dozen years of stalking human targets he had never left a contract unfulfilled. His reputation as a death machine was almost legendary, and for his crew he had selected others like himself. None of them had ever let a client down.

Until this time.

They never should have lost the prisoner, dammit. There were no such things as accidents, and no mistake was unavoidable if all security precautions were observed. His soldiers had been negligent somehow, and they had paid the price for carelessness. So it was the Cowboy's job to salvage something from the mess.

He was a skilled professional and he had put his reputation on the line. The record did not mean a thing this time. If he lost this one, he lost everything.

But he was not going to let any half-assed hit-and-run guerrilla ruin everything that he had spent a lifetime working for.

It was a long way from Jersey City where a scrawny, battered child had run the streets, surviving through an overdose of wits and nerve. He learned to fight, steal, eventually kill with the efficiency of a survivor. And in between the lessons, there were endless hours spent in darkened movie theaters, the boy in a trance as giants acted out his fantasies upon the screen.

He liked the Westerns best, with independent loners as the heroes, their law erupting from the barrel of a gun. He watched them, memorized their movements and began to emulate them, learning how to make it work for him through trial and error. As he grew older he changed, chameleonlike, and was reborn.

He had become the Cowboy.

And he headed west.

Detroit. Chicago. Phoenix. San Francisco. Anywhere that death could be translated into dollars. He selected targets like a bounty hunter tracking outlaws through the badlands, and it mattered not at all that his employers were the heavies of the piece. Technique counted even more than cash, and he had earned a reputation for his sense of style.

He was an artist, justly proud of his achievements.

This new assignment had bothered him at first. In his fashion he had always been a loyal American, but circumstances altered cases. For the kind of money he was making now, the Cowboy did not care who paid him.

The Cowboy had a duty to himself and Uncle Sam had never raised a finger to assist him. Any claim his country had on him had long ago been paid in full.

The gunman cherished no illusions as to who and what his current employers represented. Foreign money, probably the Eastern bloc. Quite possibly the Soviets themselves.

And he had hesitated—long enough to count the zeros on his first retainer check—before he made the deal. Money was what mattered. Money and a sense of style.

Recently, his jobs had been undemanding. Three hits in nineteen months, and none of them provided any sort of challenge.

As the Cowboy understood it—and he never made a practice of examining a client's motives—the targets had been low-ranking corporate employees who had stumbled onto classified material by accident. When they decided to go public or put a price tag on their silence, someone dropped a dime and called the Cowboy.

He had made the first one look like suicide, the other two like accidents. There had been no problems.

Until now.

The mark this time was a wild card. The killer did not know or care where this maverick had come from, who he was. The problems of identity and motivation were beyond his province, something to concern his clients in their lavish offices. For now the Cowboy only needed to know his target's general whereabouts, his avenue of flight. With that in mind, a careful hunter could project his track and intercept him.

Cut him off at the pass.

Just like in the movies.

Granted, this was no ordinary pigeon. Two of the Cowboy's men had learned that the hard way, and there were others at the plant, from what he understood. The guy was hell on wheels—but he was human, too.

Human and hurting.

He could dodge them in the fields, but only temporarily. The Cowboy had men and mobility. His troops controlled the roads. His prey would be obliged to take a chance, venture out into the open in order to escape. He would need a car, a telephone, a weapon—any sort of human contact. It would take a miracle to even out the odds, but he would be compelled to try.

And when he did, the Cowboy would be ready, waiting for him. Waiting to snap up the bastard.

The Cowboy sucked thoughtfully on his cheroot. He had no illusion that it would be easy pickings. He had lost the target once, and two men in the bargain. He had been at this game long enough to know that wounded animals could be more dangerous when cornered.

No, it would not be easy. But he would pull it off. The messages delivered via mobile phone had made it clear to him that nothing but death would be acceptable. Someone at the top was sweating bullets, and the Cowboy's life was riding on the outcome of his hunt. If he blew it. . . .

He put his mind in neutral, letting the tension slide away. There was nothing to worry about, no cause for alarm. He had every angle covered and sooner or later the target would show himself, provide an opportunity to finish it. The Cowboy had a hunter's patience and he would resist any pressure from above, refuse to let it rush him into careless error. There had been enough mistakes already. He could not afford another.

Mentally he started ticking off the odds against his prey—as much to reassure himself as anything. The mark had been running for two days now, exposed to heat and cold and without shelter. Food would be another problem. And in his weakened state, the prey would be intent on nourishment, a place to hide. When he was weak enough from hunger and exposure, then he would become careless.

Relaxing in the air-conditioned Continental the tracker watched the fields of green and gold slide by at fifty miles an hour. He settled down to wait. Forty-eight hours and counting. It would be soon now. He was sure of it, and he needed that certainty to keep himself together.

His troops were running quadrants to the north and east, exploring narrow side roads and checking in by radio every fifteen minutes.

So far there was nothing to report, but they were narrowing the arena and pinning down potential cover. Up to now, the hiding places had been few and far between. A culvert here, an old, abandoned shanty there. The obligatory two-bit farmhouse every dozen miles or so.

Shifting on the custom leather seat, he ground out the thin cigar and eased a hand inside his Western jacket, feeling for the stainless Smith & Wesson .44 beneath his left arm. You could drop a grizzly with that piece, probably an elephant—and for god-damned sure a wild-assed warrior who had tangled with the wrong folks this time. Drop him dead and deep, and get him off the Cowboy's back forever.

All they had to do was find the bastard.

Nothing to it.

Like hell.

He snared the walkie-talkie from the seat beside him, raised it to his face and keyed the red transmitter button. Momentary static crackled at him, quickly died away.

"Hunter One calling Hunter Two. Report."

A tinny voice broke the momentary silence.

"Hunter Two."

"What have you got for me?"

"We're coming up empty."

The Cowboy snapped his fingers at the gunner in the nearest jump seat, waited briefly while a county map was handed over. It had been divided into sectors, each approximately square and outlined on the map in yellow marker. He studied it for several moments, finally raised the radio again.

"I want another sweep on sector nine before you pack it in. You finish there, regroup on me at, ah, co-ordinates Victor Charlie seven."

"That's affirmative, Hunter One."

"Hunter Three, come in."

"We're reading you."

"Talk to me."

"Just about to put the wraps on sector five. We've got another farm to check, and then we're done."

"Don't rush it. Take your time and do it right."

"Roger that."

"And keep in touch."

"Ten-four."

He laid the radio aside, turned his full attention back to the checkerboard landscape flashing past his window. The sun was sliding toward the horizon, and the shadows in the fields were growing longer, capable of hiding many secrets.

The Cowboy could feel it. They were getting closer. He could sense the runner somewhere nearby, and they would find him soon. It was inevitable. It was necessary.

On his own another night would kill the target or permit him to escape and neither was acceptable. The Cowboy had to bring him in alive or dead, secure the only evidence his clients would accept as proof. It was all or nothing now, and he did not intend to take the place of one that got away.

He settled back, attempting to relax and very nearly making it. The features of his narrow face had settled into something like a scowl. The hunt was coming to a close.

And he could smell blood already.

4

"I need your word. No noise."

Bolan sat astride the woman, shackled hands covering her mouth, his knees pinning arms against her sides. Big frightened eyes never left Bolan's face. The breath from her nostrils was hot and frantic on his hands. He could feel her trembling beneath him, heart hammering against her rib cage like a frightened bird's. And there was something in the combination of her closeness and vulnerability—a sort of healthy sensuality—that assaulted his senses, stirring him, even now.

The warrior killed that train of thought, reminding himself that he was an intruder here. He brought the peril with him.

She was nodding in agreement to his offer, in rapid jerky movements. Cautiously he raised the manacled hands, but kept them poised to stifle any sudden scream. Finally satisfied that fear and curiosity would keep her silent, Bolan moved away from her and let her rise.

He was winded by their brief encounter, and that reminded him of his depleted strength. He sat down heavily, his back against a rough support beam, close enough that he could tackle her in case she tried to run.

She sat up facing him and tried to catch her breath.

There was color in her cheeks that could have been
produced by fear, excitement or exertion. He noted
that the panic was receding in her eyes.

"You're a fugitive."

Her eyes were on the bracelets, and it came out as a
statement rather than a question.

"I'm running," he agreed, "but not from the
police."

She raised an eyebrow.

"Those are handcuffs."

Bolan raised his hands and gave the manacles a
shake.

"Dime a dozen," he responded. "I'll be leaving
just as soon as I can get them off."

The eyes were thoughtful now but the fear was still
behind them, lurking in the background. She studied
his face, then her gaze slid lower, past the cuffs, to
fasten on the rusty stain beneath his arm.

"You're hurt."

"I'll make it."

But even as he said it he wondered if he would.

The lady shifted restlessly, leaned closer to him
with her elbows on her knees.

"You say you're running, but who from, if not the
police?"

"Not important," Bolan answered. "You don't
want to meet them." Hesitation for an instant, then
he asked her, "Have you got a car?"

"A pickup. It won't get you far."

"I may not have that far to go."

The noise alerted him. At first it was just a crack,
and the soldier could not tell where it came from.

Silently he cursed the carelessness that had permitted anyone to get so close and yet be undetected. If he had not been intent upon the woman....

The sound repeated, this time from behind and to his left. And the warrior knew that he was trapped. Bolan realized the woman heard it, too, and she attempted to disguise the sudden rush of hope that appeared on her face. Too late she checked the darting movement of her eyes, the soft lips twisting into an expression that was neither frown nor smile. Relief? Bolan wondered.

He knew that if he turned around he could observe the cavalry arriving, someone from the farmhouse coming to the lady's rescue.

Or it might be someone else that neither one of them would recognize except as Death.

In either case the Executioner could not afford to sit and wait. He might be slowing down in mind and body, but he was still a long way from surrender. As long as the man in black could think and move, there was no place for stoic acceptance of defeat.

If his time was coming, then the Executioner would meet it standing up and fighting back.

There were two exits from the loft, and Bolan knew that whoever was in the barn would approach from the ladder side. The other was an open loading bay, equipped with block and tackle, which afforded him a twelve-foot drop to hard-packed ground below. Either way could lead him into sudden death, so he chose the line of least resistance.

His eyes locked with the woman's for an instant, and he was surprised at what he found there. Sadness, and a concern that overshadowed fear, almost transforming it into unexpected sympathy.

He broke that burning contact, surging to his feet before the enemy could show himself. He broke for the hatch, the gleaming rectangle of daylight beckoning him, enticing him on.

He covered the thirty-odd feet, calculating whether to try to seize the pulley rope with lifeless fingers or propel himself into a risky freefall, landing in the paratrooper's fetal curl. He had perhaps a heartbeat left to make the crucial choice.

He was almost to his jumping-off point when the world exploded in his face. Confined within the loft, the shotgun blast was deafening. Before he could react to the report, a storm of pellets struck the wall and floor in front of him, chewing up the ancient lumber with their impact. Splinters stung his face and hands, drawing blood in places, and the sudden cloud of dust was stifling him.

Bolan slid to a halt on the treacherous footing, lost his balance and went down on one knee. When he opened his eyes, he was looking back across the woman's shoulder toward the ladder and his new assailant.

A determined-looking older man was visible from the armpits up, supported by his elbows on the dusty floorboards of the loft. He wore a denim shirt and coveralls. Steely eyes were fixed on Bolan from beneath a wide-brimmed straw hat.

But it was the double-barreled 12-gauge shotgun that commanded Bolan's full attention now. Smoke was curling upward from the starboard tube, its silent mate regarding him like an emotionless, cyclopean eye. At this range, there would be no missing any man-sized target. Even if he spun away and tried to make a break for it. . . .

The farmer seemed to read his thoughts and recognized the momentary indecision. The man broke the ringing silence with a voice as rough and weathered as the face.

"Try it if you like, boy," he said. "But make your peace before you make your move, because I'll definitely blow your ass away."

"GODDAMN DUST."

"Be quiet, will ya?"

"Look, I told you he was prob'ly shooting at a fox or something."

"Goddammit, shut up!"

Crouched between the rows of corn, Hunter Two experienced the same impatience that was troubling his lieutenant. It was ten minutes since they had heard the shotgun blast and still no one appeared outside the dilapidated barn. The gunner concentrated on observing every detail of the scene laid out before him.

It probably *was* a fox, or maybe just a rat. These country hicks would blast away at anything that moved. But Hunter Two could not afford uncertainty. He had to check it out and satisfy himself.

More important, he would have to satisfy the Cowboy.

They had left the Caddy parked at the turnoff to a narrow unpaved access road. Afraid the rising dust would reveal their whereabouts, Hunter Two had posted two sentries with the car and led his second-in-command on foot for half a mile across the fields until they found the barn and farmhouse.

They had seen a dozen houses like it in the past two days, and all of them were starting to resemble one another—rusty screens across the windows; faded, peeling paint; shingles missing from the roofs.

Hunter Two's lieutenant shifted restlessly. He was just about to speak, but changed his mind upon a warning glance from his boss. He settled back onto his haunches and slid a hand inside his jacket, drawing reassurance from the holstered hardware.

Someone was emerging from the barn and Hunter Two raised his compact binoculars, focusing across the fifty yards of intervening open ground.

A woman in her thirties, wearing jeans and some kind of work shirt with the sleeves rolled up above her elbows, occupied his field of vision. Someone else was moving out behind her now, and Hunter Two felt the breath catch in his throat. He scanned the second figure up and down, his eyes devouring every detail from the boots and tattered, bloodied skinsuit to the handcuffs on swollen wrists. The profile, smudged with dirt and drying blood from several minor cuts, was resolute, impassive.

The hunter had his prey.

An easy shot at fifty yards with nothing in the way to spoil his aim. No sweat. Beside him, his lieutenant had the Browning Hi-Power automatic in his fist, the hammer back and ready.

"Let's waste 'em."

"Not yet, dammit."

There was something out of place, a factor unaccounted for.

The gun.

Behind their mark, another man emerged from cover, bringing up the rear. He held a double-barreled shotgun at his waist, the twin muzzles leveled at the runner's spine. He was marching their fox toward the farmhouse like a prisoner of war. Whatever had gone down in there, the bumpkin was not taking any chances with his uninvited visitor. In front of them, the chickens scattered before the small procession.

"Hell, man, let's hit 'em while we've got the chance."

The hunter quickly ran down alternatives, then turned on his second-in-command.

"Just shut up, and pass me the radio," he grated.

There was anger and confusion in the eyes that met his own. For an instant, it seemed the gunner might attempt to challenge him, but then he broke the eye lock, muttering beneath his breath as he stowed the Browning, and handed over the walkie-talkie.

"Calling Hunter One." He kept it to an urgent whisper. "Hunter One, come in."

A brief delay, then: "I read you, Hunter Two. What is it?"

"Pull the flankers in," he snapped. Now the mirthless grin was back in place. "We found him."

5

A woman was waiting for them on the porch, examining them each in turn with anxious eyes. Bolan sized her up at a glance: the faded gingham dress and spotty apron, graying hair cut short to frame a face devoid of makeup. She carried aromas of a country kitchen, and the ladle in her hand confirmed that they had interrupted her in preparation for the evening meal.

She was studying the man in black—his bruised and battered face, the manacles, the bloodstains on his side. Bolan offered her a weary smile, and she returned it as a sort of twitching grimace. When she spoke at last, it was to Bolan's captor.

"Jason? What is it?"

"I caught this fella hiding in the barn. And none too soon for Toni's sake."

The younger woman blushed, the sudden color flaming in her cheeks.

"Nothing happened. Really."

Both of them were looking at her closely, and she felt the scrutiny, her embarrassment growing by the moment.

"Listen, both of you. I'm fine." She hesitated, some of the assurance fading from her voice. "He was asleep and I surprised him. I . . . fell down."

An awkward silence settled in around them, stifling further conversation. The farmer and the older woman—husband and wife, Bolan guessed—were exchanging glances, each uncertain what should happen next. Thankful for the brief pause, for the chance to catch his breath and organize his thoughts, Bolan made no move to break the stalemate. He could use the time.

Finally, after moments that had seemed to drag interminably, it was the farmer's wife who broke the silence.

"Better come inside," she said to no one in particular.

The younger woman, with a final glance at Bolan, followed the other's retreating figure through an open door. Bolan felt the shotgun muzzle prodding his spine and he fell in step behind them, his captor bringing up the rear. The soldier found himself inside a rustic kitchen, with the sink and sideboard on his left, a stove and old refrigerator to his right. The dining set—consisting of a squarish table and four straight-backed chairs—stood directly in his path. He noted that the table had been set for three, and something very like a stew was simmering on the stove. Through another open doorway Bolan glimpsed a portion of the family room.

He was calculating angles, weighing probabilities. He mentally measured distance—to the nearest window, or the parlor door—and knew the odds were all against him. In his present shape he would not have a chance unless his guard was taken out of action. Still....

He spied a rack of carving knives above the sideboard, polished blades reflecting artificial light with satin softness, and at once he dismissed the thought.

The Executioner had come to hide, not kill. He sought a temporary haven, not a killground. If a hostile hand was raised against the farmer and his family, it would not be Mack Bolan's.

The 12-gauge nudged him from behind.

"Take a seat over there where I can keep an eye on you," the farmer ordered.

Bolan chose the place without a plate or silverware and settled gratefully into the wooden chair. Exhaustion overtook him instantly; he felt the last reserve of strength evaporate, as if a giant magnet underneath his feet was dragging him down inexorably.

The farmer took up station opposite, his back against the sideboard, with his shotgun leveled from the hip. His wife, as if uncertain what to do, had gone back to her cooking. From the parlor doorway he could feel the younger woman watching all of them, confused and frightened by the grim tableau.

"You just stay put," the farmer cautioned, "while I get the sheriff over here. I reckon he'll be glad to see you."

Bolan nodded.

"That's the best idea you've had today," he said.

The farmer hesitated, plainly startled by his captive's quick agreement to the thought of calling in the law. But he recovered swiftly and reached for the wall phone with his free hand. All the while his shotgun never wavered its bead on Bolan's chest.

Perhaps the farmer could protect himself and his

family from what was coming if he called the law. But Bolan knew the sheriff could not guarantee protection against the hunters who were stalking him. If anything, confinement in the local jail would only place his life in greater jeopardy by making him a helpless, stationary target. His pursuers would not hesitate to kill an officer or two—a dozen, if it came to that—in order to retrieve him.

If it came to that.

But he was looking for another option, clinging to the knowledge that while life and hope remained he had a chance. A slim one, granted, but a chance.

To live.

To break away.

To fight again.

Without official sanction now, he was a renegade, and there was no one he could call for help. Whatever was accomplished here, the Executioner would have to do on his own.

If he got the opportunity, he would make a break during the transfer—before the local lawman had a chance to check for warrants.

Any answer out of Washington would raise some eyebrows at the courthouse, right. And Bolan did not plan to be around for any of the awkward questions that were bound to follow.

"Damn!"

The farmer finished dialing for a second time and listened briefly, then returned the telephone receiver to its cradle with an angry flourish.

At his side the younger woman asked, "What's the matter, dad?"

He made a sour face.

"Danged phone's gone dead," he answered.

Bolan felt a sudden chill along his spine. It might have been a draft—or something else entirely, intangible but every bit as real.

"You have that trouble often?"

Three suspicious pairs of eyes were focused on him now. The woman seemed more startled than afraid; the farmer glowered at him, raised the muzzle of his gun until it was in line with Bolan's chin.

"It happens, time to time," he said. "What of it?"

Right, the soldier asked himself, what of it?

"Nothing." He shrugged.

Rural telephones were famous for their shabby maintenance and lapses in performance. He was jumping to conclusions now, beginning to imagine enemies where none existed. Blind coincidence could not be overlooked, and yet. . . .

The Executioner had not survived this long by trusting to coincidence. A little paranoia could be healthy for a warrior in the field. It might be all that kept him breathing from one lethal moment to the next.

The farmer's wife was having trouble concentrating on her stew.

"It was working fine this morning," she announced.

"Never mind, Emma."

The farmer turned away from Bolan long enough to glance outside the kitchen window. It was growing dark, the afternoon declining swiftly into twilight. Clearly, what he saw did not improve his humor in the least. He faced Bolan with a frown that bordered on a scowl.

"I'd drive you into town myself—"

"Jason, no!"

"Except the pickup has a problem in the wiring. Blasted headlights don't work."

"Dad—"

"We'll have to keep on trying with the telephone," he told them all. "And if we can't get through tonight, I'll have to take you in tomorrow morning."

Bolan felt the momentary tension slide away from him. There was something ominous about the prospect of a night ride with the farmer. In his mind he saw the darkened highway blockaded by the crew wagons, the wink of muzzle-flashes as the gunners found their range.

It would be safer in the house—at least as long as he was not discovered there.

And that brought the telephone to mind.

As if attuned to Bolan's thoughts, the farmer said, "We'll try it every twenty minutes till we raise somebody, then—"

"Suppose we don't?"

"How's that?"

The younger woman's question had confused him, sidetracked his train of thought.

"Raise somebody," she explained impatiently. "Suppose we don't? Suppose the phone is out until sometime tomorrow?"

The farmer's grim expression indicated that he had not ignored the possibility. He answered her without a moment's hesitation.

"Then I sit up with our visitor tonight and drive him to the sheriff in the morning, like I said."

At the stove, his wife had now abandoned all pretense of cooking as she watched him with a pinched expression, plainly worried.

"Jason, you need sleep. You can't stay up all night just watching him."

"I'll cross that one when I come to it." Then he let a hint of softness creep into his tone. "What's keeping supper?"

"Almost ready."

"Wait a second now, dad," the younger woman interjected. "You're overlooking something: this man's hurt and bleeding, maybe seriously injured."

"He was moving pretty spry a while ago," the farmer countered, skepticism heavy in his voice. "I figure he can last the night."

"And if you're wrong?"

She plainly sensed his momentary indecision, boring in to the attack.

"He needs medical attention, dad."

The farmer cocked an eyebrow, looking dubious.

"Law says that we're supposed to hold a fugitive until the sheriff picks him up. There's nothing that requires we nurse him back to perfect health before we hand him over."

She matched the older man's determination with her own.

"It's the Christian thing to do," she said. "Besides, you don't want anything to happen while he's in your custody."

"I'm not about to be his nursemaid."

Sensing victory, she made it easy for him.

"You won't have to lift a finger. Mom and I can handle it. Some iodine and bandages—"

"I have a bullet in my side," Bolan told her. "Near the surface. It deflected off a rib. I'll take it out myself if you can get me out of these."

The soldier raised his hands and gave the cuffs a shake, surprised at how much energy the effort cost him.

"Never mind," the farmer snapped. "We'll leave 'em where they are."

"I'll get the bandages," the younger woman said, retreating out of sight.

Then the farmer's wife left the stove and brushed past her husband.

"She'll be needing help."

When they were alone, the farmer moved closer to Bolan. His shotgun stretched across the dining table, muzzles hovering a foot from Bolan's face. The voice was low and level when his captor spoke.

"Reckon I can't argue with what Toni and the missus said. But hear me plain, young fella: I was with the First Marines in World War II. I did my share of killing, plus some extra, in the South Pacific. And if you've got any thought of trying something slick, believing I won't shoot you where you sit, you're wrong. Dead wrong."

The soldier understood and never doubted him. Not even for a second.

6

After some debate, the parlor was converted to a makeshift operating room. On the coffee table were arranged the tools that Toni Chadwick required for minor surgery: a razor blade, tweezers, adhesive tape and gauze for bandages, a pan of water, iodine and rubbing alcohol.

Bolan and Toni were alone. The farmer and his wife had retreated to the kitchen. Bolan could hear them speaking in muffled tones over supper. From time to time they tried the telephone.

It bothered Bolan to plan alternatives. Whatever was responsible the breakdown in communications left them isolated, temporarily cut off from any outside contact. Which was fine—unless the enemy had somehow managed to determine his location.

If they came for him tonight....

Toni's voice was a welcome interruption of his dismal speculation.

"Lie down over here."

Gingerly, he sat down on the sofa, then stretched out on his back. The young woman knelt beside him. Her air of confidence, so evident before, was fading fast as she examined Bolan's wounds close up.

Cautious fingers brushed against his ribs, withdrew when he winced.

"Why...I mean, who did this to you?"

"Enemies," he told her. "They'll try harder next time."

"Next time?"

"They're after me, and you don't want to meet them, Toni. I'm a danger to you here."

"There's nothing I—" She hesitated, looking startled. "How'd you know my name?"

"Your father mentioned it."

"He's not my father. They...." She faltered, started over. "The Chadwicks—Jase and Emma— are my in-laws. I've been with them since...my husband died. They're all the family I have."

Bolan heard the pain behind her words and passed it off. He had no time to waste on sterile speculation.

"The sooner I get out of here, the better it will be for all of you," he told her earnestly.

She understood him, and he could see her grappling with the problem. But Toni shook her head, and when she answered, Bolan thought he recognized a hint of genuine regret.

"I'm sorry. I'll do anything I can to help you while you're here, but I can't let you go."

"I understand," he said. And meant it.

The lady resumed her examination of his side wound, looking for an angle of approach. Bolan solved it for her, raising both arms above his head. The movement stretched his abdomen and drove a wedge of agony between his ribs. He stifled a groan, but when Bolan looked again at Toni Chadwick, he could see his suffering reflected in her face.

She was bending toward him, looking closely at the blood-encrusted fabric and the torn flesh visible beneath. After some tentative probing, she tried to peel back the cloth and grimaced as it stuck fast to his skin.

She sliced the fabric with the blade and threw it back, apologizing for the pain it caused him. Bolan remained silent, but his look urged her to get on with it.

Toni gently bathed the wound, then swabbed the area with cotton soaked in alcohol. It stung, but Bolan braced himself against the greater pain to come.

He had been through it all before, in hospitals and under battlefield conditions. More than once—in Nam and later, in his urban jungle wars—he had extracted bullets from himself without the benefit of anesthetic. It was possible, with practice and determination, to temporarily divorce the mind from the reality of pain.

Bolan felt the razor's sudden fire in spite of everything, supplanted by a new sensation—deeper, more intense—as she probed with the tweezers. After a few moments his ears registered the *clink* as she deposited the bullet in a waiting saucer.

She started cleaning out the open wound with alcohol, and it was burning fiercely now, but Bolan clenched his teeth and made no sound.

"It needs some stitches. And there's going to be a scar."

"No problem."

Right. The Executioner could bear his scars, had borne them all his adult life. They were only decorations in his private war, each one the legacy of battles he had walked away from, graphic signatures of a survivor etched on living flesh for all the universe to see.

There were tears in Toni Chadwick's eyes as she finished stitching up his wound and dabbed away the final remnants of blood.

And after Bolan's wounded side, the rest was easy.

On his thigh, the bullet graze was superficial. Toni cleaned out the shallow gash, but there would be no need for stitches. Bolan painfully lowered his arms again, allowing her to clean and check his bloodied wrists as best she could with the manacles in place. Toni attended to his badly chafed skin, then coated the raw, blistered areas with ointment.

The relatively minor pain was like a dose of smelling salts to Bolan; it revived him, driving away the fog that had been threatening to cloud his mind.

The combined effects of pain, fatigue and blood loss were encroaching on the soldier's brain. He needed food and sleep, a chance to mend, but Bolan knew that he would have to settle for whatever came his way.

He was in no position now to call the shots.

Not yet.

Her ministrations completed, the woman rocked back on her haunches and surveyed her work with shining eyes.

The Executioner was very conscious of her closeness, of her scent. Soft, feminine and vibrantly alive.

"Well, I suspect you'll live," she said, almost bashfully.

"I never doubted it."

But there were doubts, all right, and Bolan knew that he was far from being out of danger. He could lose it—*all* of them could lose it, right—at any moment. The hunters were still out there, scouring the darkness, searching for his trail. Unless he moved, they were bound to pinpoint him sooner or later.

Bolan's time was running out, and there was nothing he could do to stop the clock.

When Toni Chadwick spoke again, she almost took him by surprise, the gentle voice a sweet intrusion on his dark and bloody thoughts.

"Feel like trying on some stew?"

Bolan nodded.

He attempted to stand up, but it was too early. Sudden dizziness attacked him and he sat down heavily, disoriented for the moment. Toni placed a hand upon his knee, and Bolan felt her warmth communicated through the fabric of his blacksuit like a mild electric shock.

And something caught, turned over slowly in his chest.

"Rest a while," she told him, "and I'll bring you something."

"Thanks," he said, watching her move toward the kitchen.

Momentarily alone, he had an opportunity to look around the homey parlor of the Chadwick farmhouse.

It was a *home*, damn right. Its parlor was a *living* room, and Bolan had no wish to bring the taint of death there.

Through the open doorway to the kitchen, Bolan could hear someone dialing the telephone. Then he heard the farmer muttering under his breath, banging the receiver down in anger and frustration.

It was still dead.

And in the sudden silence, he was conscious of the former chill returning.

Bolan was afraid it might already be too late. For all of them.

7

"We want it taken care of quickly."

"So do I." The Cowboy's knuckles whitened as he gripped the mobile phone receiver. "I also want it taken care of *right*. No more accidents, no more mistakes."

There was a momentary silence on the other end. He took advantage of it to explain himself.

"I haven't had a chance to reconnoiter the terrain. We get some light, I'll check it out and lay an angle of attack."

"How complicated can it be?"

The Cowboy recognized the sarcasm, but chose to ignore it.

"I'm not committing any troops until I have a feel for their defensive capabilities. We haven't even got a head count yet. That hick could have an arsenal in there."

"If you are unable to handle it—"

"I'll handle it, all right," he snapped. "*My* way, in my own time. I wasn't hired to rush these jobs and screw things up."

"Perhaps you need some help."

"I need some room to breathe. Some time to think this out. You wanna push it through tonight, pick out a crew and come on down. I'll pull my men and let you have it to yourself."

"We have the utmost faith in your professional ability."

So far. It was not spoken, but he heard it all the same. There was a stiffness, a formality about the other's voice that telegraphed his anger, barely in control. The Cowboy thought he heard a trace of a foreign accent.

"When can we expect results?"

"Tomorrow sometime, at the latest."

"No loose ends."

"Relax, they're bottled up. Nobody's going anywhere."

"All right then. I shall look forward to your call."

And the link was broken. He looked at the telephone in his hand, restraining the initial urge to slam it down. Now more than ever he needed iron control to stifle anger. Too much feeling was a danger in his chosen line of work. Emotion bred mistakes and made a soldier vulnerable to his enemies. There had been too many foolish errors already; he could not afford another.

Visibly relaxed, he keyed the walkie-talkie to find his pointmen in the darkness.

"Heads up."

"I read you, Hunter."

There was boredom in the small, metallic voice.

"What's your situation?"

"Nothing to report. They're showing lights, but no one's poked a head outside since we came on."

"Stay put and keep your eyes peeled," he instructed. "I'll have someone relieve you in an hour."

"Roger that."

He set the radio aside and spent a moment staring at the darkness, grappling with his doubts. The situation was not evolving as he had expected. There were vital pieces missing and he had to find them before he risked his men on a rash assault.

He had expected some reaction when they cut the phone lines, isolating the occupants of the farmhouse. Logically, the Cowboy's target should be in the ancient pickup truck and on his way to town right now, under guard. It was the natural next step.

Except that something had gone sour along the way.

He started ticking off alternatives, attempting to anticipate the farmer's every move.

There was a chance—a slim one, granted—that the runner might have overpowered his captor and seized the shotgun. The Cowboy dismissed the thought. If his prey had turned the tables by acquiring armament and transportation, he would be long gone by now. Remaining at the farm was tantamount to suicide, and there was nothing self-destructive in the runner's moves so far.

There had to be another reason why the farmer would prefer to hold his captive here, instead of handing him over to the authorities.

It was a narrow alley going nowhere, and the Cowboy finally gave it up. The information would reveal itself with daylight; in the meantime, there were preparations to be made.

The Cowboy would be ready when his opportunity arrived. He was not leaving anything to chance. It had to be perfect the first time. No mistakes. No foul-ups.

He left the Continental, wincing at the momentary brilliance of the dome light, and joined his soldiers. They were waiting for him, clustered by the cars, invisible from any distance in the darkness. It was still an hour to moonrise, and the only light available was the glow of half a dozen cigarettes.

The little caravan was parked along the narrow access road that linked their target to the highway. The Cowboy's Lincoln was sandwiched between the carbon-copy Cadillacs, the three tanks blocking off the track effectively with gunners to complete the seal.

The troops were getting restless, chafing at the long delay. He read it in their posture, in the way they watched him, waiting. And he faced them each in turn, projecting all the confidence and self-assurance he could muster, willing them to share the hunter's patience.

A disembodied voice addressed him from the gloom.

"What's the word?"

"No change. They're sitting tight."

Another voice: "Okay, let's take 'em."

"That's a negative."

Momentary silence, then a murmur rippled through the ranks. He sensed the confusion, mingled with resentment, radiating from the men that surrounded him. The nearest gunner put it into words.

"We've got it covered. What's the point in waiting?"

"That's the point: to be damn *sure* we've got it covered."

No one answered. They were waiting for him, and he moved into the silence with authority.

"We need their numbers, troops and weapons. Stumble in there blind, you may bite into something sour."

"I counted three of them, with one old shotgun." That from the scout who had run their prey to earth.

"Uh-huh," he countered, cold as ice. "But I don't recall you checked out the house."

He felt the iron control returning. They were his again.

"We can't rule out the possibility of other hands around the place," he told them. "And I never knew a farmer who felt right without a half a dozen guns to keep him company."

"They should have moved him out by now," a trooper said to no one special, voicing the confusion that had plagued them all.

"I can't account for the delay," the Cowboy told them honestly. "They have to hand him over eventually, and we'll be waiting when they make the move."

"All right."

"I want to take out some insurance. Give our side a little edge."

"Like what?"

He smiled.

"Like some of that C-4 we brought along."

"You wanna blow the house?"

"It's not exactly what I had in mind."

And he explained the plan in simple terms, assigning roles as he rehearsed it. By the time he had finished, they were satisfied, at ease. They knew his plan would work if each man performed his part precisely.

It was time to send the starters in.

"You'd better take the C-4 and get it rolling. Have the pointers cover you, then send 'em back."

"It's done."

The gunners split off in groups of three and four to smoke and talk in whispers. He was satisfied to let them iron out the rough spots among themselves.

The Cowboy ambled off in the direction of the farmhouse and his target. Make it plural now, his target*s*. He could not permit a living soul to leave the farm when they were finished with their business.

He had not survived this long by being soft or sentimental. Although he had nothing personal against the farmer or the woman, they were obstacles that had to be removed at any cost. If left alive, they could identify him to authorities.

The Cowboy no longer cared why the farmer was waiting. Let him stall for daylight if he chose; the end result would be identical. There would be no escape.

They were in it now, and there was no way out but through the Cowboy. Younger, better men had tried that route before, and had come to grief in the attempt.

Beyond the whispering rows of corn, his quarry was invisible, but he could feel them with a hunter's sensitivity. He touched them with his mind, and knew that he could take them any time he wanted to.

Still, the hunter waited. He had them under siege, and none of them were going anywhere. The Cowboy could afford to give them one last night on earth.

What he could not afford was careless overconfidence, the kind that killed his gunners in the transport vehicle two days ago.

This time it would be a simple job, if everybody followed orders to the letter. Just like taking candy from a baby.

Make that three babies, one of them armed—at least—with a double-barreled 12-gauge scattergun.

That changed the odds a bit, of course, but five to one was more than good enough.

The Cowboy settled down to wait for sunrise.

8

"More?"

Bolan shook his head and pushed the empty plate away.

"No, thanks. I'm fine."

Seated opposite Bolan in an easy chair, the shotgun resting on his knees, Jason Chadwick pinned him with a probing stare.

"I reckon all that hiding out works up an appetite. How long's it been since you ate?"

"Two days, give or take."

"Well, I expect you'll eat more regular in jail."

"Dad, for heaven's sake!"

The farmer looked at his daughter-in-law evenly, without expression.

"No harm in telling things the way they are."

And Toni was about to answer back when Bolan interrupted her.

"I meant it when I told you that I wasn't running from the police."

"I heard you, fella. But you *will* admit those bracelets are a mite suspicious."

Toni chimed in suddenly, surprising both of them.

"I don't think those handcuffs mean a thing."

The farmer looked at her with new eyes, clearly startled.

"Are you taking up for him?"

The dark eyes flashed from Bolan to her father-in-law and back again. Uncertainty was written on her face.

"It's not that. I just think we ought to let him tell his side, that's all."

The farmer shrugged.

"I'll be glad to listen, s'long as everybody understands the sheriff has first claim on him."

"We may not have the time to wait for reinforcements."

"What's that supposed to mean?" asked Jason Chadwick, looking at Bolan.

"Some people are after me, all right, but strictly unofficially. And they won't be taking any coffee breaks until they find me."

"Some kind of gang, I'd guess, supposed to break you out."

"Supposed to bury me. And anyone who's been in contact with me."

The farmer remained silent for a moment, finally spoke.

"It seems to me you'd want police protection. 'Less, of course, you're hiding something."

"There's no way your sheriff can protect me now."

"That so?" Jason made no effort to conceal his skepticism. "Those must be some rough old boys. You mixed up with the Mafia or something?"

The Executioner suppressed a sudden urge to laugh

out loud. He never once considered telling everything, or even the majority of what he knew. Much better if he kept it clean and simple, to preserve his shaky credibility, if nothing else.

And he could hardly hope for Jason Chadwick and his family to accept the whole, unvarnished truth. The average mind, untrained and unattuned to dealing with the underworld of criminals and saboteurs, would find the facts bizarre, implausible. Bolan took the path of least resistance as he answered Jason's question.

"Something like that, yes."

The older man was watching him, and Bolan could almost hear the brain at work behind his captor's eyes.

"I guess you'd better start at the beginning, boy."

Bolan took a moment, putting all his thoughts in order, to make sure his story had the ring of truth before he started speaking.

"I have information that could damage them, upset their plans. They can't afford to have me talking. I'm a risk, and so is anyone I've been in touch with. Anyone at all."

He had not meant to glance at Toni then, or frighten her unnecessarily, but he could see the color draining from her cheeks. The younger woman seemed convinced of Bolan's story. She was terrified, and no mistake.

"Is this where I'm supposed to get all green around the gills and let you walk right out the door?"

"It wouldn't be a bad idea," he told the farmer earnestly.

"Not bad for you, at any rate."

"The truth is, I was thinking of your women," Bolan said.

"Uh-huh."

Bolan glanced at Toni from the corner of his eye, and saw that something in her face had changed—the fear transformed into a kind of sympathy, perhaps— and he knew she was afraid for him, as well as for her family and herself. It was a victory of sorts, but Jason and his wife were clearly undecided, still suspicious of his story.

And why not? He was asking them to take the word of some pathetic fugitive above their own best instincts. In their place, he, too, would be skeptical. And he could read the answer in his captor's face even before the farmer spoke aloud.

"I'll have to let the sheriff sort this out." And to his wife, "Why don't you try the phone again."

She left then, returning in less than a minute, shaking her head.

"Nothing," she reported.

"Damn! I've got a mind to take it out of next month's bill," the farmer groused.

"I hope you're still around next month."

The farmer's hand had come to rest on the shotgun's trigger guard.

"We'll have no more of that. I won't be threatened in my own damn house."

"The threat's outside," Bolan said. "Or it will be soon."

There was a moment's thoughtful silence, but Jason Chadwick's face remained passive.

Nothing was to be gained from arguing, and Bolan let it go. He was already thinking past the moment, looking for an out that would involve a minimum of conflict with the Chadwicks. Given half a chance, he could disarm the farmer. He would fight back, and Bolan would be forced to kill or injure him before he left the farmhouse.

At the moment, it was not a viable alternative.

Later, perhaps—when the bloodhounds were closer—he might be forced to violence. But if there was any chance at all of slipping out without a fight. . . .

The Executioner was not afraid of any man, but early in his Asian war he had acquired a simple code. In a ruthless war without frontiers or boundaries, he clung steadfastly to his principles, which distinguished him from others of his kind.

A soldier gave his word of honor sparingly—and having given it, defended it to the death. No matter if the word was given to a friend or enemy, Bolan stood by it but never hid behind it.

Bolan would never take up arms against soldiers of the same side, even when a tainted individual betrayed his trust and dabbled in the slime of treason. Bolan left collection of their cosmic debts to other hands; his own had blood enough to bathe in.

Bolan had become the Executioner in Vietnam, and simultaneously he earned the nickname of Sergeant Mercy: on one hand, a coldly efficient killing machine; on the other, a warm human being who would go the extra mile and risk his life, his mission, for the sake of wounded comrades or civilians.

Only an extraordinary man could carry both

names well, and Bolan pulled it off with style. He
found no contradiction in his opposite roles of savior
and destroyer. In Bolan's view, a warrior necessarily
embodied facets of them both. He was employed to
kill, but only so that others could survive. When
savages encroached upon the gentle civilizers, then it
was a soldier's lot to stand behind them and to stem
the tide.

It was a blood tide, and sometimes—too often—it
swept away the soldier's sense of balance, dragging
him under. Until he lost himself completely, reemerging in the perfect likeness of his savage foe. It took a
special kind of fighting man to stand his ground, and
although the Executioner was not unscathed, he had
seen it through with heart and mind intact.

So far.

Sometimes it was too much for a single man to
bear, damn right. But Executioner Mack Bolan did
his part, secure in the knowledge that other hands
and hearts shared his burden. He was separated from
his former allies now, by geographic space and proc-
lamation of their mutual commander, but the warrior knew what they were going through from one
day to the next.

The man in black had been there, right, and after
getting into it, he found there was no easy exit from
the hellgrounds. Life and death were simple on the
surface, but behind the bare mechanics, motivations
ran together in kaleidoscopic chaos, unless you kept
your full attention on the guideposts.

Duty.

Honor.

Justice.

Love.

The love of life itself, as life was meant to be. Dynamic. Fruitful. Growing.

There were times when love of life conferred on a man the right to kill. If a soldier turned away, allowed the savage foe to work his evil in the world, then that warrior was as guilty as the cannibals themselves. He was a traitor to the universe that gave him life.

In the final analysis, the Executioner would have his scars to show, but he would never stand accused of treason.

Movement close at hand distracted Bolan, roused him from his momentary reverie. The women were clearing off the dinner remnants, getting ready to retire. Jason Chadwick kept his seat across from Bolan, both hands resting on the scattergun. The gaze he turned on Bolan showed a mixture of emotions: curiosity, suspicion and the smallest trace of fear.

And Bolan finally recognized the fear of injury to loved ones, felt the infant tremors that had just begun to undermine his captor's iron resolve.

The farmer had been listening to him, after all. He was not buying all of it—perhaps not any of it yet— but he was thinking. For the moment, it was victory enough.

So long as Bolan had the moment.

Normal kitchen sounds were audible beyond the doorway, and again he felt the stark duality of his surroundings. He was an alien in this world, and his presence was changing those around him, gradually but forcibly inducting them into another world they did not understand. The women were engaged in their routine domestic business while a manacled guerrilla occupied their parlor and their father-husband kept him under guard.

As Bolan's gaze took in the domestic scene around him, an unfamiliar feeling was conceived deep in his soul. He tried to tag the edges of this undefined signal, give the flag substance, but the wavering image fell in and out of focus, finally eluding him.

The nameless embryonic sensation continued to gnaw at his gut, frustrating every futile attempt to pin it down. Then his migrating thoughts began to hold steady and he had it.

Family.

Damn right.

Bolan realized it was the presence of the double-barreled 12-gauge in the farmer's hands that triggered the dormant alarm. Like a panning camera, Bolan's thoughts crossed the lifetime from Pittsfield to the present. And the yearning for his family threatened to consume him like fire.

In Emma and Jason Chadwick, Bolan saw his dead parents. And Toni Chadwick reminded him of his sister, Cindy. But the picture was incomplete. An integral part of this homey pastiche lay missing.

Johnny.

Where was he now?

He would no longer be in the custody of Val Querente, Bolan was certain. And if the true Bolan blood coursed through his brother's veins, then Johnny would more than likely be on his own by now.

As Bolan's racing thoughts gained momentum, he knew that his decision to stay away from Johnny was sound. There could have been no other way. And through the years, even though Bolan ached to see his only living kin, no amount of loneliness could shake his resolve. The Executioner would never allow cannibal man to threaten the scion of the Bolan clan.

It would have been easy to locate Johnny through Leo Turrin. But any attempt to effect a reunion would have endangered the boy's life.

Boy? At that thought a smile cracked Bolan's trancelike mask. Johnny was a young man by now. What did he look like? Had his life run an easier course than The Executioner's? Bolan hoped so. Any other way would be too much to even contemplate.

Bolan longed to tousle his younger brother's hair, toss a few in a game of touch football, reel in some rock bass from a clear mountain stream. And yes, catch up on the years that had separated them.

Suddenly, Bolan made a decision. When this was all over, if he survived, he would look for Johnny.

Bolan would find his blood.

The Executioner was wrenched back to reality as his gaze fell on the twin snouts of the 12-gauge shotgun pointed at him.

He recognized that Jason had it in him to become a killer, indeed, *re*-become; the man had paid his dues and done his duty in another war. Alone among the Chadwicks, he had caught a glimpse of Bolan's world, but that was long ago and far away.

It would remain to see if he could find the fortitude for here and now.

9

While the Chadwick women finished their K.P. duty, Jason turned his full attention to the problem of securing his prisoner for the night. The Executioner saw consternation mingled with determination on his captor's face.

"I mean to keep you company tonight, but still...."

He hesitated briefly, seemed to hit upon a sudden inspiration.

"Emma, will you step in here a minute?"

Hesitant, still toweling soapy hands, his wife appeared in the open kitchen doorway. Jason turned to face her.

"I need that chain we used to use on Buster. And the extra padlock, from my toolbox. The keys are with it."

Emma Chadwick nodded without answering and turned away to fetch the items. Her eyes met Bolan's for only a heartbeat, but he had time to read a sampling of the mixed emotions there. Above all else, the fear was dominant.

When it came down to fear, they had only scratched the surface. Except perhaps for Jason and his fading memories of hell in the Pacific, they knew nothing yet of mortal terror.

Bolan hoped that none of them would ever have to learn what they were missing.

Emma Chadwick returned, carrying a length of slender chain and a small padlock. She placed the items on the table.

"I don't plan to fall asleep," he told the Executioner, "but accidents can happen. Wouldn't want to see our company run off without the chance to say goodbye."

He passed the 12-gauge to his wife, and she took it with an obvious reluctance, holding the weapon away from her body. Jason picked up the lock and chain and crossed the parlor to stand in front of Bolan.

"Get up a second, and I'll get you situated," Jason ordered.

Bolan rose and watched the farmer as he dragged the sofa several feet along the wall. One end of it was now adjacent to a tall cast-iron radiator, and at once Bolan understood his captor's plan.

"Sit down."

The farmer waved him to a seat beside the standing heater. The man in black obeyed instructions, took his place without an argument.

Swiftly, Jason Chadwick looped the slender chain through Bolan's handcuffs, passed one end of it through grillwork on the upright radiator, and secured the loose ends with his padlock. It would take some practice, but the Executioner had enough room to stretch out on the sofa.

"I know this won't hold you if you've got a mind to leave," the farmer said, "but that old heater's pretty solid. It'll take some work to pull that grating loose, and there's no way to keep it quiet.''

And he was smiling as he took the shotgun back from his wife, settling into his easy chair again.

"You get some rest now, fella. Reckon you'll be needing it come morning."

Bolan was determined not to sleep. He would remain awake, alert to any sound inside or out, in case the hunters tried to storm the house during the night. Within the limits now imposed on him by circumstances, he had to be prepared for anything.

His captor lasted barely ninety minutes, and by midnight Jason's muffled snoring filled the parlor. Bolan watched him sleeping fitfully, aware that he could never reach the shotgun without waking Jason.

Bolan's tether was too short to let him cross the living room, although he found that he could stand and move about within a six-foot radius. But if the trackers found him now, while he was fettered like a watchdog on a leash, it would not be enough.

Another hour, and fatigue was challenging determination, bottomless exhaustion chipping at the soldier's iron resolve. His catnap in the loft had not refreshed him, and he felt the soft, seductive arms of sleep enfolding him against his will. He was nodding, drifting. . . .

It might have been a moment or an hour, when a small sound awakened Bolan. The years of training, living on the edge, had served him well, and he was scanning for the source of a potential threat before he was aware of having been asleep.

The sound was close, muffled, like the surreptitious closing of a door, and he was conscious of another presence in the living room. A scent. . . .

Bolan made the recognition and relaxed at once. The presence was familiar, even welcome, and it held no menace for him.

Toni Chadwick stepped into the feeble light from Jason's low-wattage reading lamp. Her hair was tousled from the pillow, and she wore a flannel nightgown underneath a belted robe. She glanced at Jason, dozing in his chair, and seemed to glide across the living room until she stood within arm's length of Bolan. When she spoke, her voice was a whisper.

"Sorry if I woke you."

"It's okay. I need to stay awake."

The semidarkness could not hide her anxious look; the shadows on her face made Toni look more worried than before.

"You really think we're in some kind of danger, don't you?"

Bolan nodded.

"Yes, I do. The worst kind."

"If you're right . . . I mean . . . what happens next?"

"That all depends on whether I get out of here before someone comes looking for me."

"If they find you here. . . ."

She had no need to finish. Bolan understood the question.

"They won't have a choice," he told her flatly, fighting down the urge to make it easier. "Every witness is a liability."

"I see."

And from the grim expression on her face, he knew

she was beginning to. The lady had started to tremble, and she found a seat at one end of the sofa, leaving ample space between them. Bolan knew that it was not from any squeamishness, but rather from a sense of elementary caution. He was still a stranger here, presumably a hunted man, and while he felt the stirrings of an embryonic empathy between them, prudence kept her at a distance.

"I don't even know your name," she said at last.

"Frank LaMancha," Bolan answered, falling back upon the alias he had used in other jungles.

For the Executioner was dead, officially. Twice dead, in fact; as Sergeant Bolan and again as Colonel Phoenix, he had sacrificed two lives and two identities.

Another shift, and he could feel the lady reaching for something, working toward it by degrees, as if reluctant to address the thing head-on.

"If there was something I could do...."

"You've done a lot already."

Momentary silence, and there was a distance in her voice when Toni spoke again.

"My husband, Jerry, was a deputy with Butler County, and he loved it. Helping people, fighting crime...or what there was of it. He used to talk about his job like it was a crusade or something, but it made him happy. We were shopping for a house, about to start a family...."

There was a small catch in her voice, and Bolan felt her on the verge of tears. He waited, let her get around to it in her own way.

"It was our anniversary—one year, a Friday

night—and Jerry got off early. He was going to pick up some wine for dinner, and he walked into the middle of a robbery in progress. They had shotguns, and...the doctors told me that he didn't suffer.''

She was facing Bolan, and despite the tremor in her voice, the shining eyes were dry.

"It's like a war, isn't it?"

Damn right.

There was no way, no need, to answer her. A sudden flash of understanding that was almost physical had passed between them. They had touched and drawn apart, but in the silence they were closer than before.

"I've got no family living," she continued. "Jase and Emma took me in, and they've been wonderful—don't get me wrong—but still, sometimes I think there must be...something else."

There was an almost wistful quality about her voice, and Bolan knew that she was opening a private corner of her thoughts to his inspection. It was a sort of intimacy, and he felt attracted to her even as he sought to remain aloof.

"You'll find it, Toni. Give yourself some time."

But Bolan knew that time could be a problem.

He did not choose to make this woman—any of these people—active members of his own crusade. But sometimes, choice became a casualty of war, and men—or women—fought because they had to, not because it was their hearts' desire.

Bolan was a volunteer but he had never loved the killing. It was necessary, even right, because it was the only way on earth to keep the cannibals at bay.

And the Executioner was not infatuated with the bloody business of his everlasting war. Provided with a choice, he might have chosen any other path and spent his life away from jungles and the predators who dwelt therein.

Except that Bolan never had a choice. Not really.

From the moment he donned a soldier's uniform, took on a warrior's duty, he surrendered many of the basic freedoms that he sought to guarantee for others.

Toni's whispered voice intruded on his thoughts.

"I really didn't mean to ramble on like this," she told him sheepishly. "I only wanted you to know that I believe your story. I don't pretend to understand it, but I count myself a decent judge of people."

"So do I," he said.

Their eyes met and once again he felt the flow of something pass between them. When she said goodnight and rose to leave, he felt a sudden urge to reach for her and keep her there beside him.

Bolan stifled it and let her go.

The time and place were wrong for weaving dreams, and he was more familiar with the nightmare side, in any case. The soft and gentle life was left to others; Bolan had devoted all his strength and energy to winning it for them. Sentiment would only slow him down, delay him when the moment came for swift, decisive action.

He had spent a lifetime fighting mortal enemies; unarmed or outnumbered he would keep on battling. The only road lay through his enemies. No detours allowed.

The Executioner would not have it any other way.

10

The first real light of morning roused him, and the soldier stirred, reminded of his wounds immediately by the fleeting pains that settled around his torso.

In a flash, Bolan remembered everything. He understood the tether that restrained him, recognized the dozing watchman seated opposite, his scattergun between his knees, the muzzles pointed toward the floor.

The soldier rose, resigned himself to angry protests from the bruises that were somehow fainter now than on the day before. Stiff, Bolan gingerly stretched himself with both arms raised above his head, alert to any sign of stress on the sutures in his side. In spite of everything, he felt rejuvenated by the very sleep that he had struggled so long to avoid.

The night was over, and they were alive. What lay ahead for Bolan and his captor-hosts was something else again.

He gave a soft, experimental tug on the chain. It held. Another jerk, with greater force this time, and he could see the grillwork of the heater start to budge. Once more. . . .

"Save your strength, boy. Never know when you'll be having need of it."

Bolan turned to face the farmer, found him upright in the easy chair. His 12-gauge was no longer pointed at the floor. Its double muzzles hovered at a point between Bolan's chest and groin, unwavering. He shrugged, and with a gesture of dismissal let the choke chain slither through his fingers.

"Worth a try," he told his jailer.

"Reckon so."

They faced each other for a moment, soldiers separated by a generation. Bloody years lay between them, but when Bolan looked at Jason Chadwick there was something like a momentary flash of recognition deep behind his eyes. This man had seen his duty once, had followed it to hell and back. He saw another kind of duty now, no less compelling, and again he answered to the call.

Mack Bolan could respect his captor, certainly. He understood the farmer, but his understanding did not change a thing.

One way or another, Bolan had to break away.

A bedroom door swung open on the farmer's flank, and Emma Chadwick came to stand beside her husband. Jason spared his wife a glance, and handed her the scattergun. She took it from him with the same expression of uneasiness that Bolan had observed the night before.

"You keep him covered, now," the farmer told her, "while I get him ready for the ride to town."

Jason Chadwick crossed the living room and stooped beside the radiator, fumbling with the padlock for a moment, finally releasing it. He unwound the chain, stepped closer to release it from Bolan's handcuffs.

Weighing angles and percentages, the soldier knew that he could pull it off. A simple sidestep, close the gap. No problem. He could use the farmer as a human shield, force Emma to discard the weapon, or at least to hold her fire while he retreated to the pickup truck outside.

As quickly as the thought materialized, he let it go. The Executioner had done enough.

The farmer had retrieved his shotgun, and he covered Bolan with it as he circled toward the open kitchen door.

"Time to go," he said to Bolan, and gestured toward the exit with his weapon. "Move it."

Bolan was turning toward the kitchen, when another door was opened at his back. He glanced around, caught sight of Toni in the doorway of the second bedroom. Her expression was a mixture of sadness and bewilderment, as if she had awakened from a morbid and confusing dream.

Their eyes made fleeting contact, but there was no time for lingering goodbyes. A jerky motion from the scattergun revealed his captor's own impatience, and the Executioner moved out of there, with Jason behind.

Outside, beyond the covered porch, it was still cool, despite the early-morning sunshine. Bolan waited at the steps until his warden prodded him in the direction of the barn. From where they stood, the tailgate of a pickup truck was visible around the corner of the barn, hidden so that Bolan had not seen it on his superficial recon of the farm the previous afternoon.

They crossed the dooryard briskly, Emma following, with Toni watching from the porch. The Executioner felt suddenly exposed, as if a dozen pairs of eyes were on him. He wondered if the trackers could have found him in the night, if they were watching as he moved across the open ground.

If they were waiting in the corn, or there—behind the barn—it could be over in a flash. A muzzle-flash, damn right, and there was nothing Bolan or his captor could do about it. One determined sniper, or a firing squad with automatic weapons, could command the barnyard from a hundred different vantage points.

Bolan waited, half expecting death—searing pain between his shoulders blades, or simply blackness as the bullet cored his brain. He wondered if the fatal gunshot would be audible before he fell and spilled his life into the dust.

He was almost surprised when they reached the truck without incident. A feeling of foreboding was upon him now, and he could not escape it. There was something. . . .

Jason's pickup was a battered Dodge. The dents and dings and peeling paint reminded Bolan of the farmhouse, of the owner himself.

"Stand up against the barn," his captor said. "I need to think this out."

The Executioner obeyed and took the opportunity to scrutinize the truck more closely. There was ample room for both of them inside the cab, but with the shotgun, Jason would be crowded, at a disadvantage. Maybe, when they reached the highway. . . .

Bolan's eyes had come to rest on the rusting hood,

and now he felt a chill along his spine, the warning tremor raising the hair on his scalp.

The hood was open. Just a fraction, as if someone had not slammed it hard enough. As if they were afraid of making noise to rouse the sleepers in the farmhouse.

Bolan made his move. He was standing at the pickup's nose, with both hands searching for the hood latch, when the farmer reached him. Sudden pressure of the twin muzzles underneath his chin forced Bolan's head back at a painful angle.

"Tired of livin', boy? Just what the hell you think you're doin'?"

Bolan kept it calm and cool.

"I thought I'd take a look under the hood."

The farmer snorted.

"Reckon I can get to town and back without a tune-up, thanks."

"We may not make it to the highway."

Silence for a heartbeat, and Jason Chadwick's eyes were scouring his face.

"You've got five seconds to start making sense," he growled, but at the same time he stepped back a pace, removed the muzzle of his shotgun from the soldier's throat.

"Your hood is open," Bolan told him simply. "Now, if you've been working on it, fine. If not...."

He left it hanging, but the farmer understood him, and his eyes were darting back and forth from Bolan to the truck, remaining longer on the open hood each time. Another moment, and he cleared his throat to speak.

"You're saying someone's been around here messing with the engine."

It was not a question.

Bolan shrugged. "No way to tell, unless we have a look."

"All right, go on. But no sudden moves. I'll be watching every moment."

Bolan found the latch, released it, raised the pickup's hood. The effort cost a bolt of pain between his ribs as he tried to manipulate the hood with manacled hands, but he finally got it to stay upright on its own. He circled to the right, the truck between himself and Jason now, as he bent closer to inspect the engine.

It took him only seconds to discover what he sought, wedged in against the fire wall of the pickup.

"There."

He pointed, and the farmer craned his neck to get a look.

"What is it?"

"Plastic explosive," Bolan told him. "Wired to blow when you turn on the ignition key."

Somewhere behind him, Emma Chadwick gasped. The farmer shot a glance at her, returned suspicious eyes at once to Bolan.

"Somebody trying to kill me?"

"Like I said, I'm the target. You're just in the way."

The farmer glanced around him at the silent fields.

"They must've hooked it up sometime last night. I never heard a sound."

"It wouldn't have taken them long," the soldier said. "You're dealing with professionals."

"Your kind of people."

"Not exactly. But we understand each other."

"Mmm. I take it they don't want the sheriff in on this." He faced the man in black, his eyes demanding. "Don't suppose they'll let it go at this."

"They can't afford to," Bolan answered, nodding toward the plastic charge. "This is just for openers; we call it, and they'll have to raise. No choice."

"It's thirty miles to town."

"We'd never make it. Backup teams are standard on a hardset. They'll have gunners waiting for you by the time you reach the highway."

Jason Chadwick stiffened, hands white knuckled as he gripped the shotgun fiercely. Anger and uncertainty were mingled on his face.

"Damn. We'd best get back inside the house."

"Agreed. But first, I need to disconnect this."

He was reaching in across the fender, stretching painfully, when Jason laid a firm hand on his arm.

"Just hold on there a second. You know what you're doing?"

The soldier nodded, hoped the little smile conveyed more confidence than he was feeling at the moment.

"Nothing complicated. But you might be smart to wait for me inside."

The farmer eyed him closely, but there was a new expression on his face, replacing some of the suspicion there. Then he turned to his wife, waving her away.

"I'll stick," he said. "You go back inside and see to Toni."

"Jason—"

"Go on now!"

Reluctantly, she left them, and as if by mutual consent, neither man spoke or moved until they heard the screen door slam.

"No point in taking chances," Jason told him simply.

"No."

And Bolan noticed for the first time that his captor's shotgun was not pointed at him anymore. The muzzles were directed skyward.

"Best get on about it," Jason said, the voice a blend of nervous tension and impatience.

Slowly, cautiously, Mack Bolan went to work.

And it was nothing complicated, right. A simple and straightforward wiring job that any demolition man might learn his first day on the job. No problem there.

Unless a sniper in the fields behind them saw what he was doing and decided it was time to bring the curtain down.

The soldier closed his mind to morbid possibilities and concentrated on the task at hand. When it was time to die, there would be no choice in the matter.

11

"A bomb?" There was bewilderment in Toni Chadwick's voice.

Bolan and the farmer had left the yard. Now they were all seated around the dining table.

"One thing's plain enough," the farmer said to Bolan. "Someone doesn't want you on the street."

"Will you believe him now?" the younger woman asked. There was a hint of desperation in her voice.

Jason thought it over for a moment, frowning. Finally he cleared his throat.

"I won't pretend to understand it all," he answered. "But I don't believe police are sneaking in and out of here at night, planting bombs in trucks."

"What are we going to do?" Emma asked.

"First, we try the phone again," her husband said.

She rose and crossed the kitchen, lifted the receiver gingerly, as if she feared it might explode. She listened briefly, jiggled the switch hook with an index finger, finally cradled it again, disgusted.

"It's still dead."

She rejoined them at the table, eyes downcast. The silence grew increasingly uncomfortable.

The lump of deadly C-4 lay before them in the center of the table. Bolan had removed the blasting cap and slipped it in a pocket of his skinsuit to eliminate the risk of accidental detonation. Close behind the brick of gray explosives lay a hacksaw, Jason had detoured to retrieve it from the barn while Bolan finished defusing the pickup truck outside.

"Reckon we can look for trouble any time," the farmer said, his voice was harsh.

"They'll likely wait for dark," the warrior told them, "but there's no sense taking chances. Someone ought to close the drapes. And stay away from windows if you can."

At a nod from Jason, both women left their seats and started drawing curtains shut across the kitchen windows. In another moment, they were moving toward the living room and bedrooms, leaving Bolan and the farmer alone.

The soldier watched his captor closely, finally raised his arms, both fists together. "I could use some hands."

"I figured."

With a sigh of resignation, Jason shifted places so that he was sitting next to Bolan. He picked up the hacksaw, studied Bolan's cuffs a moment, finally brought the narrow blade to rest across the manacle.

The tempered steel in Bolan's handcuffs was resistant to the blade, but finally Jason Chadwick freed Bolan's left arm, started on the right. A second blade was needed to complete the job, but after forty minutes Bolan was released and felt the life returning to his cramped and aching hands.

The women had returned, and Toni flashed a little smile at Bolan as she moved to help with breakfast. The kitchen was alive with sounds and smells of food in preparation. The Executioner believed that he had never savored any smells before with such intensity; it seemed impossible that reeking death would dare intrude upon that small domestic scene.

But one glance at the molded plastic charge, squatting in the middle of the breakfast table like a dark, malignant growth, was all it took to bring the warrior back to reality.

Breakfast arrived at the table, piping hot, and Bolan quickly swept the C-4 out of sight, deposited the charge beneath his chair. He had no fear of an accident; without the blasting cap, plastique was eminently stable. But he knew the innocent-looking lump beneath his seat could easily have totaled Jason's pickup truck or taken out the front half of his farmhouse.

With any luck at all, Mack Bolan figured he might be able to make use of the explosive himself.

Confronted with the ample breakfast spread, he ate ravenously. Finally he pushed his empty plate away.

"I swear that sleeping makes you hungrier than running," Jason said, and he was smiling for the first time since their gunpoint confrontation in the hayloft.

"Everything was perfect. Thank you," Bolan told the women.

"We've got work to do," Jason said to no one in particular.

"They'll have the numbers on their side," Bolan said. "We need an equalizer. Are there any other guns around the place?"

"I've got a .22," the farmer told him, "but I haven't used it in a coon's age."

"Nothing else?"

Jason Chadwick shook his head ruefully.

"I never went in much for hunting."

Bolan looked around the kitchen, and his mind was seeking alternatives, a way to make up for the firepower they lacked. The rack of kitchen knives he had observed earlier would not give them any range. And it if came to fighting hand-to-hand, he feared they were lost.

The soldier reached beneath his chair, retrieved the lump of plastique. He weighed it in his palm, already calculating the defensive and offensive possibilities.

"We'll get some mileage out of this," he said. "I wish we had a few more blasting caps."

Across from him, the farmer banged an open palm against the tabletop, making both women jump.

"We've got 'em!" he declared, excited now. "I had to blow some stumps last fall, and there were two or three caps left over."

Bolan felt a cautious surge of hope. The time factor could be a problem, certainly, and Jason's caps might prove defective from exposure or old age—but it was still a chance.

"Where are they?"

"In the barn." The farmer scowled, remembering the danger outside. "I didn't want them in the house." Another hesitation, then, reluctantly: "I'll fetch 'em in."

Bolan raised a cautionary hand.

"Hold off a while." The military mind was racing now, envisioning a makeshift fortress where the house had stood. "We'll need some other hardware if you've got it."

He started running down the checklist, pausing periodically while Jason mulled availability of items and suggested an alternative from time to time. When they were finished, Bolan felt he had the makings of his fortress well in hand.

If he could find the necessary hardware in the barn and bring it safely to the house, escaping the hunters waiting for him in the fields outside.

They had a chance, but only that. Success would now rely on luck and on the jungle fighter's skill in almost equal measure.

And he had a plan. But it required the soldier to transform himself. He took it one step at a time.

"I could use a shower."

Jason looked at him as if he doubted Bolan's sanity, but something in the warrior's face and manner stilled his questions.

"Soap and towels are in the bathroom."

Bolan thanked him, rose and left the breakfast table. He could feel their eyes on him as he cleared the kitchen door and passed into the living room, finally out of view.

Inside the little bathroom, Bolan closed the door, not bothering to lock it. Gingerly he peeled the skin-suit off and dropped it in a corner.

When he finished cleaning up, the soldier would require a change of skin. It was a necessary part of the facade.

He turned on the shower, adjusted it until the heat was slightly short of scalding, finally stepped inside the tub. He let the stinging spray wash over him, the rivulets removing grime accumulated during two days in the fields. At first, the water pooled around his feet was murky, but after several moments it ran clear again.

After a few minutes, Bolan cut the hot water off and switched to an icy spray that left him shivering and wide awake. It drove the final cobwebs back and out of mind, removing any drowsiness his sleep had left behind.

He was reaching for the knob to turn the water off when Bolan heard the bathroom door swing open softly, close again. Jungle instincts sprang to action, and he whipped the plastic shower curtain back—eliciting a startled little cry from Toni Chadwick.

Standing there, a stack of neatly folded clothing in her arms, the lady took in everything at once and quickly turned away with flaming cheeks.

"I'm sorry. Really, I—"

"Forget it."

Toni never saw the grin that softened Bolan's face. He killed the water, snared a towel from the rack, and snugged it tight around his waist like a sarong.

"This isn't me. I mean, I don't go barging in on men in showers." Toni hesitated. "Are you decent?"

"More or less."

Her eyes were on the wound in Bolan's side, a little worried frown upon her face. She reached out for him, caught herself, withdrew the hand. Self-consciously, she offered the clothing. Bolan saw a denim shirt and overalls, some underwear.

"These are Jason's," she explained. "The fit may leave a lot to be desired, but still...I thought you could use a change."

"Thank you."

Toni made a little gesture of dismissal, shifting restlessly from one foot to another as she stood in front of him. Unconsciously, her eyes were wandering across his chest and shoulders, studying the musculature and the patchwork pattern of his battle scars. A moment later, realizing he had caught her at it, she was coloring again, retreating toward the bathroom door.

"I guess that's everything," she said.

"I guess."

The silence stretched between them, making Toni even more uncomfortable, and Bolan finally let her off the hook.

"I'll only be a minute. Thanks again."

As she closed the door behind her, Bolan's face relaxed into another smile. Some kind of lady, right, for damn sure.

In another time, another set of circumstances—

Bolan cut it off before the fantasy could put down roots. There was no time for gentleness or rest and recreation in this hellground.

Moving briskly, grimacing in silence at the lancing

pain between his ribs, he started dressing. Another kind of uniform—and Toni had been right about the fit—but it was what he needed at the moment. With a little luck, it just might be enough to see him through.

12

"You really think this'll work?"

"It's worth a try. Besides, I may spot something we didn't think of."

Bolan gave a final tug to the suspenders of his borrowed overalls and snugged the straw hat on his head. The sleeves of the work shirt were rolled to his elbows, but there was nothing he could do about the high-water cuffs of his pants. Close up, he was a gawkish parody of a farmer, but at a distance....

"Don't expose yourself," he said to no one in particular, "but keep an eye out. There's a chance I may need cover fire on the return trip."

Jason made a jabbing motion with his shotgun.

"I'm on top of it," he promised.

"Okay. It's going to take some time, but I'll be back as soon as possible. If I run into any opposition, you'll be hearing from me."

He left them in the kitchen, lined against the window, and crossed the covered porch. Emerging into morning sunlight, Bolan hesitated on the wooden steps, his narrowed eyes adjusting once more to the glare. For what he had in mind, the soldier needed every operating sense at full efficiency.

It was a daring plan, fraught with peril, but the Ex-

ecutioner was far from reckless. He had calculated
odds and angles, tried to weigh the variables before
determining his course of action. In the end, he could
not come up with any viable alternative.

He was relying on "role camouflage," a talent first
acquired in Vietnam and later polished to an art form
in the urban jungles.

In Nam, the Executioner had once been trapped
behind hostile lines, cut off from all communication
with his comrades. Cornered, he had donned a coolie
hat and black pajamas, crouching in the middle of an
open rice field while the Cong patrolled the roads
around him. Through an endless afternoon he waited, with a hundred pairs of savage eyes surrounding
him, until the twilight offered him a chance to slip
away. And while the soldier should have been picked
out at once, betrayed by stature as a foreigner, no
enemy had challenged him. The savages had seen
what they'd *expected*, overlooked the infiltrator in
their very midst.

With any luck at all, he just might pull it off again.
No need to squat for hours in the open now; it was a
simple walk, no more than forty yards from house to
barn, and it was harder to identify a moving target
every time. But still. . . .

He cast a final glance around the barnyard, taking
in the silent fields on either side. The corn could hide
a multitude of snipers, any one of them prepared to
cut him down—but Bolan had surrendered choice the
moment he left the shelter of the porch.

The fact was unavoidable; he had to go ahead.

He pulled the hat brim lower, making sure to keep

the movement casual as he put his face in shadow. Slouching to take inches off his height, the warrior moved out, ambling across the open ground as if he had nowhere to go and a lifetime to get there. Attitude was half the battle if he meant to carry off his daring ploy.

Before he took a step, the military mind was reaching out ahead of him, anticipating obstacles and dangers.

Jason had seen no one in the barn that morning, but he might have missed a silent sniper in the hayloft. Likewise, there had been time and opportunity enough for the hunters to install a team to the barn after Bolan had defused the Dodge and took their burden inside the house.

They could be waiting for him in the barn, yeah, and if they were....

Then what?

There would be nothing he could do about it, other than to warn the people in the house. If ambushed, he would have to make his dying loud enough that Jason and the women could prepare themselves for an attack. He had to let them have that chance.

And even as the thought materialized, he shrugged it off. The Executioner was nothing if not realistic, and he knew the farmer's family would be dead without him. They had seen and heard too much by now for his pursuers to show any mercy. Their only chance for living lay with Bolan—and the jungle fighter knew that chance was slim enough already.

Bolan was halfway to the barn when he heard the screen door bang like the crack of a pistol shot against its frame. Bolan froze. Then he heard the sound of running footsteps closing on him from behind. Toni Chadwick called to him, attempting to disguise the tension in her voice.

"Uncle Jason, wait for me!"

The soldier cursed under his breath, and turned to face her. There was nothing he could do out there on open ground to turn her back without revealing his intent.

"I'm glad I caught you." Toni's face was flushed, her breathing heavier than brief exertion justified. "I'll walk with you."

Stiffly, covering his irritation with an effort, Bolan nodded, pivoting and continuing in the direction of the barn. The lady fell in step beside him, looped an arm through his, a carefree woman in the company of a favored older relative.

But her aptitude did not soften the soldier's anger. All the odds were out of kilter now. If they walked into an ambush, it would be impossible for Bolan to protect her.

He was conscious of the prairie sun above him, beating down on his head and shoulders, baking into him. He had the sudden feeling of a specimen beneath a magnifying glass. He shook off the feeling of defeatism as they reached the questionable safety of the barn.

Inside, the sudden shade was cool and soothing. Bolan stood rock still for a moment, combat-ready eyes surveying the interior. He scanned the stalls, the workbench, searched the loft as best he could from down below.

As far as he could tell, they were alone.

He turned to Toni Chadwick now, his face and voice a study in control.

"You should have stayed inside," he told her simply.

"Don't be angry." Toni's manner bore no trace of meek subservience. "I couldn't let you come out here alone."

"You might have killed us both. If someone had been waiting here—"

"I thought of that," she interrupted him, determined. "And I knew it didn't matter. If they kill you, they kill us all."

Hesitation, and the lady's voice was softer as she finished with a question.

"Do you really think we've got a chance?"

He nodded solemnly, suppressed a sudden urge to reach for her and draw her close against him, shelter her.

"We do," he answered, "if we can be ready for them when they hit. I wouldn't want to pick a favorite, but we've got a chance. Just that—no more."

"Ouch." She grimaced. "You don't pull your punches."

"We're in this together," Bolan told her. "You deserve to know the odds."

"Okay." She straightened, shoulders back. "Let's get started."

Bolan found a gunny sack beneath the workbench and began to fill it with the items from his shopping list. He bagged a hammer and a five-pound box of roofing nails, a pair of wirecutters, and a twenty-foot electrical extension cord.

The bale of chicken wire was where the farmer had predicted, and although Bolan had been hoping for barbed wire instead, he thought it would be adequate to serve his purpose.

From a shelf above the workbench, he retrieved a dusty lantern with perhaps a pint of kerosene inside. And finally, rounding off his survey, Bolan chose a sickle and an ax from the assorted tools, deposited them in his bulging sack.

He turned to find the lady watching him intently, with a kind of sick expression on her face. Her eyes were focused on the ax protruding from his bag.

"I don't know if I can handle this," she told him candidly.

"You'll handle it," the Executioner assured her. "When the action starts, there isn't any time to be afraid."

She hesitated, eyes downcast, embarrassed, like a penitent preparing to confess her sins. The soldier sensed a conflict going on inside her, and he did not push, preferring that she get around to it in her own way and time.

"I wish we had more time," she said at last. "To talk, and... get to know each other."

"This is all the time there is."

"I know that, dammit."

And the lady stepped into his arms, her own around his neck as she surprised him with a burning kiss. The soldier hesitated for a second, conscious of her body pressed against his, the electric charge that seemed to surge between them, then his own arms closed around her tightly.

They clung together for a long, loving moment, and the Executioner was first to break the contact. He held Toni away from him, looking deep into the shining eyes. He saw the desire in her face and something in himself responded ardently, but caution born of battlefield experience restrained him.

"Toni, listen—"

"No," she told him flatly, interrupting. "You said it yourself; this is all the time we have. Tonight we may...." She hesitated, swallowed hard around the knot of fear and tension in her throat, and tried again. "I don't intend to waste my last few hours by denying what I feel."

He looked at her and understood the yearning that so often gripped combatants on the eve of mortal conflict. Something in the human animal demanded it, an affirmation of survival in the face of violent death.

And was there more to it than that? The soldier neither knew nor cared. He shared the lady's urge, her primal passion.

"They're expecting us inside," he said, and knew before he finished speaking that it sounded lame.

"So they are."

She was unbuttoning the woolen shirt and shrugging out of it, presenting Bolan with a little glimpse of heaven. Nervous fingers took the belt and zipper of her jeans by storm, and as he watched, she peeled them off and stepped away from them.

The combination of reserve and animal abandon in her attitude was stirring Bolan, whipping at his senses, and almost before he knew it he was struggling out of Jason Chadwick's overalls.

They stood together and Bolan gathered her into his arms. Bolan could not mask the grimace of pain from his recent wounds as the lady locked her legs around his waist. But the pleasure surmounted anything else he felt in the fevered moment. Bolan entered with a driving thrust that wrung a gasp of pleasure from them both. She matched his ardor, wriggling, straining, head thrown back and fingers clenched into the muscles of his shoulders.

The moment was too fiery, their passion too intense to be prolonged. Within seconds of each other they exploded, clinging desperately together.

Afterward they did not move, reluctant to forsake the warmth of human contact. Toni shivered, not from any chill, and Bolan felt her tears upon his shoulder. When she spoke, her lips were pressed against his chest, the words a muffled whisper.

"God, it's been so long. There's been no one... since Jerry."

Bolan's heart went out to her. He was well attuned to loneliness of soul and body, to the loss of someone close enough to be a part of him. The jungle fighter had been through it all, in spades.

He knew what she was feeling, right. They had much more in common than the momentary sharing of some private space.

"I know it's crazy, everything considered, but I'm glad you're here."

"So am I."

He felt the power returning, and the lady felt it, too, her dark eyes widening in surprise.

Toni let herself accommodate his movements,

picking up the tempo on her own. The dance began again and both of them surrendered to it, lost in one another.

They were alive, damn right. And if the night, another hour, found them otherwise, they would have this to carry with them into darkness everlasting. The delicious friction of their coupling struck a spark, their labored breathing fanned it into flame no hostile shadow could extinguish.

Bolan and the lady were alive, and living large. Together.

If it came to that, their dying would be large, as well.

13

"We could have taken them, no sweat. They were sitting ducks, but you said—"

The Cowboy interrupted his observer, and he made no effort to conceal the irritation in his voice.

"I know what I said. Get on with it. What were they doing?"

"Cleaning out the barn, from what I could tell. They took some things back with them to the house."

Involuntarily, a muscle started ticking in the Cowboy's jaw.

"What kind of things?"

The spotter shrugged. "Nothing special. Just a hopsack—I couldn't see inside it—and a pitchfork. Oh, some kind of chicken wire or something—in a roll, you know?"

A murmur ran through the troops, and the Cowboy waited for it to die down before he spoke again.

"That's all?"

"Uh-huh."

Someone on his left cleared his throat in preparation for a question.

"What is this? I mean, what the hell would they be doing with a bale of chicken wire, for cryin' out loud?"

The Cowboy scrutinized him for a moment, leaden eyes invisible behind the mirrored glasses, and another of his soldiers beat him to the answer.

"Shit, it's obvious. They're going hard."

There were sporadic chuckles, but a growing number of his guns appeared uneasy at the prospect.

"We ought to get in there and mop 'em up before they have a chance to lay an ambush for us," came a fourth voice. "If we do it now, we could just walk on in—"

"And get your ass shot off," the Cowboy finished for him. Scowling, he surveyed the ring of sullen faces. "A daylight rush is something we do not need. Right now, we've got them under siege, outnumbered and cut off. I don't intend to give up that advantage just because a few of you are getting sunburned."

The Cowboy listened to the uneasy muttering again, but mixed with cautious laughter now. The heat of early afternoon was working on them all. But they were professionals, and he was confident that he could hold them in formation.

"We could drop a couple of cocktails on the roof," somebody ventured from his right. "Burn the house down and pop 'em when they run out."

"If they do," a grinning comrade added.

"Great idea," the Cowboy told them. "While you're at it, let's send up some flares to go along with the smoke signals, shall we? Wouldn't want a fireman in the state to miss it."

"What's the story, then?"

"The story hasn't changed," their leader snapped,

allowing another flash of anger to show through. "We wait for nightfall, and we take them according to the plan. No fuss, no muss. And no damn signal fires out here to draw the cops like moths around a candle."

"I wonder how they tumbled to the plastique," someone asked.

"No matter. It was worth a shot. Forget it."

"Better not forget who's got it now."

The Cowboy flashed a grin devoid of humor.

"What's C-4 to them?" he asked. "It might as well be Silly Putty. Hell, I hope they try to rig it up and do us all a favor."

The Cowboy was in control again. He could feel it. They would follow orders, he knew, as long as they possessed an illusion of participation.

The Cowboy was a natural leader, with a talent for manipulating his subordinates.

But now, in spite of every possible delay, the time had come to deal with his superiors. And something told the gunman that they would not be so understanding or so easily manipulated as his button men.

The Cowboy was supremely confident of his ability, but confidence was not contagious. His employers had been shaken by the man in black, and nothing short of his annihilation would put their minds at ease. They were already chafing at his overlong delay, unable to understand why he waited once the target was in sight.

The Cowboy scowled as he climbed inside the Lincoln. These were different men, unlike the others he was used to working for. He was accustomed to the mobsters and the *mafiosi*, men who killed or hired killers in pursuit of monetary profit. These the Cowboy understood, because their motivation was identical to his.

But with his new employers, there was a difference.

Beneath the businesslike facade, he sensed a certain dedication to a cause that marked them as fanatics of a sort. He had done business with their kind before, of course—the wealthy headcases and professional haters who refused to get their own hands dirty. He understood them, to a point, but they were unpredictable if someone stepped on their obsession.

Reluctantly, he snared the mobile telephone receiver, buzzed the operator, waited while she patched him through. A rough, familiar voice responded.

"Yeah?"

"It's Hunter. Is he there?"

"Hang on a sec."

After several moments another male voice on the line, softer, but with steel beneath the velvet.

"Yes?"

"I'm checking in with nothing to report. The party's scheduled for tonight."

"We are uncomfortable with the delay."

"It's unavoidable. I want to take the guest of honor by surprise."

"It seems a little late for that."

He read the condemnation in the other's voice, but the Cowboy forged ahead, undaunted.

"That was just a fluke. Somebody got their signals crossed is all. We're ready for him this time."

"I hope so."

"Don't worry about it."

"I have to. Nothing can proceed until you take delivery."

"It's as good as done."

Momentary silence on the other end, finally broken by the graveyard voice.

"We cannot tolerate another failure, Hunter. Be advised."

"I understand."

"We knew you would."

The line went dead, and he was quick to cradle the receiver, anxious to sever the polluting link. He wondered what it was about his late employers that made him feel unclean.

The message had been crystal clear, at any rate. The Cowboy had to bring his quarry in or become the hunted. There could be no third alternative.

He thought of it as an incentive rather than a threat, and there was no fear in him. Every job was life or death, without exception, for the quarry and the hunter. He was not afraid of targets that could shoot back, and he gave his all to every job regardless of the promises or threats from his employer.

Still, it rankled him to have these foreigners insult him, treat him like a common soldier. When the job was done—and after he had pay in hand—the Cowboy would be pleased to teach them all a lesson.

It could advance his growing reputation if he handled it correctly, and encourage future clients to regard him as the true professional he was. The Cowboy smiled, reflecting that he might be able to pick up some money on the deal if he could find a patriotic backer who would pay to have him do what he intended to perform for nothing.

The hunter stopped himself, returned his full attention to the problem. He had a contract to fulfill, and he had fumbled once—no, twice—already. Two strikes gone, and on the third one he was out. All the way.

He shifted mental gears, now concentrating on the runner and his temporary hosts. It mattered little if there were three people or a half a dozen in the farmhouse. Either way, they all belonged to him, and he would have them soon enough.

It was amusing to imagine them inside there, busy trying to defend the indefensible. A fortress made of chicken wire, defended with a blunderbus and pitchfork. It was enough to make him laugh out loud, and he surrendered to the moment as he left the Continental.

The troops were watching him suspiciously, no doubt concerned about the sanity of anyone who started laughing in the present circumstances. Never mind. They were proficient at their work, but none possessed the full capacity to understand his feelings.

He checked the sun's position overhead, confirmed the hour with his Rolex. Several hours yet until the darkness came to cover his advance. An afternoon of waiting, watching.

The Cowboy turned and recognized the wheelman standing closest to him, called him over.

"I make it thirty miles to town."

The driver nodded.

"All right, you take a couple of these heroes in and get some burgers—whatever. Something cold to drink. Keep it soft."

"Okay."

The driver turned away, retreating toward the final car in line and beckoning to some of his colleagues as he left. Two of them were handing over their automatic weapons to the others, moving toward the Caddy, climbing in.

The Cowboy let them go, dismissed them from his thoughts. They would obey instructions because they feared his anger. And they would return with food and soft drinks, passing up the liquor stores and bars for now, because they knew anything that slowed their reflexes on the eve of combat could be fatal.

The hour was coming, slow but sure, and every man among his troops would be prepared, primed to kill on sight.

He thought again of those inside the weathered farmhouse, huddled in the shadows and preparing their defenses. Let them do their best; in the long run, it would not extend their worthless lives an hour. If anything, it made the game more interesting for the hunter.

He considered it a challenge, and the Cowboy knew that he was equal to it. He was looking forward to the final play with grim anticipation.

14

Bolan finished stripping down the rifle and arranged its parts along the coffee table, ready to begin a piece-by-piece examination. The weapon was a Winchester Model 90, the most popular slide-action rifle ever made and a genuine classic. Although production was discontinued in the thirties, thousands of the guns were still at large. But Bolan had not seen or handled one since boyhood days in Massachusetts.

Assuming that the one in his possession was among the last produced—a perilous assumption in itself—the rifle must be more than fifty years old.

He sighted through the twenty-four-inch octagonal barrel to satisfy himself that there were no obstructions. There were enough inherent risks in the coming battle without having his weapons detonate and blind or kill him when he fired the opening shot.

Finally satisfied, the soldier turned his scrutiny to the rifle's other components, wiping down each part in turn with strips of oily cloth before he reassembled them.

Bolan raised the slender Winchester, found it almost feather light compared to all the military hardware he was used to. A single fluid motion brought the weapon to his shoulder. He swept the muzzle in a wide arc, settling on a clock above the mantle. Bolan pumped the slide action smoothly, squeezed the trigger gently in a practice fire. The hammer fell, impacting on the firing pin with a resounding snap.

Bolan rested the rifle in his lap, then reached across the table and retrieved the single box of rimfire ammunition Jason had been able to locate. He shook the container experimentally, frowning as he upended it and spilled the little cylinders of brass onto the table, counting swiftly.

Seventeen rounds of .22-caliber Long Rifle ammo lay scattered in front of him.

Seventeen cartridges.

Fewer than two dozen.

They were newer than the rifle, certainly, but still of unknown age and dubious reliability. Under the circumstances, he could not afford to waste a single one of them in test fire, or for sighting in his weapon.

It would have to do.

He thumbed a dozen rounds into the tubular magazine beneath the barrel, pumped the slide to bring a round into the firing chamber. Carefully, he eased the hammer down and set the safety, finally topped the magazine off with a thirteenth rimfire cartridge. Just for luck.

The .22's effective range was tabulated at a mile, but he was counting on a firing distance of less than thirty feet. No matter where the enemy attempted to invade their little bunker, he would be inside the soldier's killing range.

The little .22 was often disregarded as a killer once the target grew beyond the rodent class, but the Executioner knew otherwise. The .22's ballistic properties made it particularly lethal. Once bullets were inside the body, ricochets were commonplace, with the tiny slugs caroming off bones and drilling channels through a dozen vital organs. A .45 or Magnum bullet might go through a human target, right, but the little .22 could turn his guts into a sieve.

Satisfied that he had done his best, Bolan pocketed the five remaining cartridges and turned his full attention to the task of finalizing his defensive preparations.

On the coffee table to his right, the soldier had arranged the brick of C-4, the lantern he had taken from the barn, several empty vegetable cans, the box of roofing nails, a carving knife and several rolls of tape.

From the pocket of his overalls, he withdrew a tissue-paper parcel and unwrapped it gently, laying out its contents on the table with his other gear. Neatly ranked before him on the table were four blasting caps—the one retrieved from Jason Chadwick's pickup and three others, which he had located in the barn. As was the case with the rimfire ammunition in his .22 repeater, there would be no opportunity for testing in advance of combat.

They would work, or they would not. But either way, the warrior had to try.

He pulled the lantern close and satisfied himself that it had been refilled to adequate capacity.

Then Bolan took the carving knife and quartered the loaf of high explosive into roughly equal segments. Three of these he shoved aside; the fourth was quickly molded to the lantern's globe, secured in place with strips of black electrician's tape. In the center of the charge, he cut a narrow slit and filled it with the newest blasting cap, tamped the lethal firecracker in its place so that a quarter inch remained exposed. That done, he cut two strips of white adhesive tape and plastered them across the blasting cap. In darkness, when the lamp was lit, the pristine cross would give him something he could shoot at with a fair degree of accuracy.

When he was finished Bolan began production of some crude offensive weaponry to complete the little stockpile. He dropped a handful of the wicked roofing nails inside each of the empty cans. Next, he stood a twist of C-4 upright in each can, and filled the space around the goop with more nails, so that a square inch of the lethal putty was exposed on top. With each in turn, he wedged an ancient blasting cap into the plastic charge, approximately half of each protruding above the rim of the can.

The lids were ready for him; each now bore a hole dead center, punched by Toni with a hammer and screwdriver. When the metal discs were fitted into place and heavily secured with tape, the primer caps extended up above the lids like lethal nipples.

Like percussion detonators, right, prepared to blow on impact, spewing twisted tin and roofing nails as gruesomely effective as the latest military frag grenade.

Assuming, sure, that he could pitch the loaded cans with any kind of accuracy under battlefield conditions. And assuming, always, that the blasting caps would blow in any case.

He left the homespun charges in a lineup on the coffee table, took the rifle with him as he rose to leave the living room. It was time to check the others, do his best to guarantee that everything was ready when the hostile troops arrived in force.

By Bolan's calculation, there was little better than an hour of light remaining. Anything they accomplished in their own defense would have to be achieved within that hour.

They were swiftly running out of time.

And with the darkness, Bolan knew, the killing would begin.

TONI CHADWICK TUGGED THE STRIP of chicken wire taut against the window frame. Then she hammered a nail in place, securing the upper corner. Yet another tug, another roofing nail, and she stepped back to admire her handiwork. When she was satisfied that it would give them warning of a break-in, she began tacking down the edges.

Standing there before the window, with the curtains necessarily open wide, the lady felt exposed and vulnerable. Her skin was crawling with the knowledge that a hostile stranger might be watching her, examining her every movement. And if that observer crouching in the corn grew nervous, if his trigger finger twitched involuntarily. . . .

Her hands were trembling, interfering with her work, and Toni put the fear behind her with a Herculean effort. In its place, she concentrated on the stranger who had stumbled in from nowhere to upset her life completely.

Frank LaMancha.

He was not entirely strange to her, of course—not after their surprise encounter in the barn. Toni felt the heat and color rising unbidden in her cheeks. For a frozen moment of eternity, they had been as close as soul and body ever could be, but at every other level he was still a mystery, exotic and enigmatic.

Frank LaMancha.

The name itself inspired a host of questions. Toni never doubted for a moment that it was an alias of some kind. Still, it seemed to fit the stranger perfectly.

A thousand different questions crowded in on her all at once, until her inner turmoil almost canceled external fear. She wanted to know anything and everything about him: who and what he was, his mission, how he came to be inside their barn in handcuffs, wounded, with a troop of killers on his trail.

LaMancha was a soldier of some kind; she saw it clearly in the way he took command as if by natural right or instinct. He was familiar with the world of guns and bombs and killing; it reflected in his eyes and in his many scars, the way he handled weapons and directed others in the preparation of defenses.

He was a professional at this, no doubt about it, but she wondered whether his ability could compensate for their inadequate supply of weapons. Take the chicken wire, for instance; while she understood the logic, Toni knew the flimsy makeshift screen would never stop a determined enemy. It would not even slow him down.

She felt the fear returning, frowned and went

ahead with it. She would complete the job because he asked her to, if for no other reason.

Strange, the way this man from nowhere had imposed himself upon her life, reviving in several hours the sensations that had been dormant since Jerry. Toni had succeeded in suppressing her desires—or very nearly so—after that abhorrent Friday night.

There were stirrings underneath the surface ice, of course, the transient throbbing of remembered love and pain, but she had been in charge.

Until yesterday.

The stranger dressed in black had literally burst her cold protective shell, a human cannonball demolishing the igloo Toni had constructed for herself. He had released a whirlwind of emotions, and the lady knew that it was too late now to duck the storm.

Whatever he had started, she would have to see it through.

Providing that she got the chance, of course. And at the moment, it was doubtful that she would survive the night.

An unexpected sound behind her startled Toni and she jumped involuntarily, striking her thumb with the hammer.

"Damn it!"

"Sorry, my fault."

Toni swiveled, found the handsome stranger watching from the bedroom doorway. Through the pain, she tried a small, embarrassed smile.

"Naturally clumsy," she told him.

The blue eyes were warm, appreciative.

"How's it coming?"

Toni stood aside to let him view her work without obstruction.

"Almost done. Besides, I'm running out of thumbs."

He smiled, surveyed the partial roll of wire and little bag of nails that Toni had deposited on the double bed.

"Have you got everything you need?" he asked.

She nodded.

"Two more windows in my...in the other bedroom. I can cover them with what I've got here."

"Good. We've got about an hour, give or take. We need to have it ready by full dark."

"I'll have it done," she promised.

"Right. I'll check in with the others, then."

And he turned away, retraced his steps in the direction of the kitchen. Toni watched him go, suppressing a sudden urge to call him back. What had she expected, anyway—a pat on the head or a kiss on the cheek?

Toni recognized that they had spent their loving time together and had seen it slip away. There was nothing to look forward to but killing time from here on. And she would have to keep her fingers crossed, to pray that she was equal to the challenge—or it might be dying time.

And for the first time that she could remember in the past two years, the lady had a positive desire to live.

JASON CHADWICK GAVE THE NAIL a final stroke, then set his hammer down atop the kitchen counter. He tried the door, put his weight behind it, but the nails held fast. The door refused to budge. And it would hold them for a while—long enough, at any rate, for him to bring the shotgun up and send a few of them to meet their maker. After that....

The farmer felt a gnawing apprehension growing stronger by the moment. It reminded him of nights in the Pacific, crouching in a hole and waiting for another human wave to break along the firing line in howling, bloody chaos. Gunfire and grenades, the roar of howitzers and reedy voices shrieking, mangled bodies thrashing in the fire-lit darkness.

He would have liked a head count of the enemy, an inventory of their armament. The house would shelter them for a while against a force with handguns, even a rifle or two. But if the hostiles came in any kind of numbers, weighing in with heavy weapons, there would be no hope of holding out for any length of time.

He glanced at Emma, busy sorting through the kitchen drawers, collecting anything that might be useful in a fight at close quarters. On the dining table, she had piled the carving knives and cleaver, an eighteen-inch barbecue fork, assorted other household tools and bits of silverware. They could strike some telling blows with that collection if the fight was hand to hand, but no amount of cutlery would stand against superior firepower.

Jason wondered what his wife was feeling, how the siege was working on her mind and nerves. There was an unfamiliar tightness in her face, around the mouth and eyes, but otherwise she went about her task as if it was an ordinary everyday event. If she had any fears or doubts about their situation, she was keeping them securely locked inside herself.

Voices reached his ears from the direction of the living room, and he frowned, reflecting on the change in Toni's attitude since their unwelcome guest had arrived.

At first, Jason had regarded it as sympathy or pity for an underdog, the kind of feeling she might harbor for an injured animal, but now he saw that there was more to it. Much more.

He had observed their faces when they came back from the barn together, and he studied Toni's mannerisms when she talked about the stranger or addressed herself to him directly. There was an animation in her face that had been missing since the night his boy was killed.

And Jason did not know if she was falling for the man in black, but there was something ill-defined and growing stronger, more pronounced. It worried him, as much as if his own daughter had just announced that she was eloping and taking off for Hollywood.

Jason wondered at his attitude, decided that his absent son was part of it. Some portion of him had assumed that there could never be another man for Toni, and he saw at once how damned irrational that was. But there was something else, beyond the pangs of posthumous parental jealousy; this man was dangerous—to Toni, all of them, and to himself.

The stranger might, indeed, have sealed their fates already.

The farmer felt protective toward his women,

granted, and he made no apologies because of it. He had been raised respecting home and hearth, the sanctity of family. And he had gone to war in the defense of certain simple values that he cherished. Four long years of hitting beaches, ducking snipers' bullets, killing faceless enemies in stinking jungles— all to guarantee that home and hearth remained inviolate.

The islands of the South Pacific were a world away, the enemy was different, but the basic issue never seemed to change. A man defended what he loved and what was his; if it cost a man his life, he paid the price and took as many of the savage bastards with him as he could.

Corny values, certainly, the love of country, home and family. In recent years, it had become the fashion to despise America, to spit on patriotism and the flag.

Jason Chadwick knew all of it was bullshit. He would never claim perfection for his country. She had faults, as did the members of his family and the man himself, but the farmer loved them fiercely, all together.

Forty years ago and more, he had been ready to lay down his life—or take the lives of others—for his country's sake.

Today, defending home and family, the farmer was prepared to kill again—or die.

And it was all the same to Jason.

Movement in the kitchen doorway drew his thoughts outside himself, and Jason turned to find the stranger standing there, surveying all their preparations. In a single sweep, his eyes took in the pile of cutlery, the screen secured across the windows, Jason's sturdy reinforcement of the door.

"It's looking good," he told them.

Jason frowned.

"We've done the best we could," he answered. "It won't hold 'em very long."

"With any luck, it may not have to."

A final glance around, and the stranger vanished back inside the living room. Jason watched him go and felt the mix of jumbled feelings stirring in his gut again.

He did not fully understand the stranger, did not necessarily trust the man completely, but he recognized their only hope of living through the night. Whatever his designs and motivations, this one was a cool professional, no doubt about it. And deep down, underneath the nagging dread and fear of death, he was damned glad to have the stranger with them now.

15

"Will this really work?"

Bolan read the doubt in Toni's voice and tried to reassure her. Cautiously.

"In theory, sure. But it's the outer line, remember that. We'll slow them down, maybe take a couple out along the way, but it won't keep them out indefinitely."

Toni nodded, and her expression told him that she understood the gravity of his remarks. She watched him nervously as he continued with his final preparations for the coming battle.

With the wire cutters he had taken from the barn, Bolan clipped the unplugged electric cord where it connected to the toaster. That done, he split the leads along the length of the cord almost to the plug. Then he smoothly stripped the insulation back a few inches from the cut and unraveled all the shiny copper wire inside. Another moment, and he determined the live strand, tying it to a corner of the makeshift screen nailed up across the window above the kitchen sink. Then he fastened the other lead to a plumbing pipe. He hesitated, stood well back in case of unexpected sparking, and plugged the cord into a nearby outlet.

Nothing happened, and the soldier flashed a little smile of satisfaction to the lady. At a glance, the screen of chicken wire looked totally innocuous, but anyone who touched it would receive a lethal jolt of current.

Windows in the living room and bedrooms had been similarly armed, connected to the stripped and severed outlet cords of household lamps. Each electric screen would constitute a circuit in and of itself; the breaching of a single window by their enemy would leave the others primed and fully operative, waiting for a deadly contact.

Unless someone outside got clever and decided to cut off their power at the source.

A glance outside confirmed that they were swiftly losing daylight, and the warrior hastened to complete his preparations. There was a single window waiting to be rigged, the broad one facing out on the Chadwick porch. With practiced moves he took the long extension cord and clipped its rubber socket off one end, removed the heavy insulation in a single fluid motion. Soon he had the cord connected firmly to the screen of chicken wire, its other end plugged in beside the toaster cable.

They were ready, except for one last detail.

Bolan took the lamp with its plastique attachment, knelt to place it close beside the kitchen door. He calculated ranges, distance and trajectory, positioning the lamp precisely. It would have to clear the door when that was breached and still be visible from his position in the living room.

When he was fully satisfied with the position of his

booby trap, the warrior raised its decorative chimney, used a wooden match to light the wick. A pungent smell of burning sulfur filled the Chadwick kitchen, and he was reminded briefly of the battle smells that linger on a killground.

Fire and battle smoke. The smell of death. A whiff of hell on earth to make believers of the living.

Delicately, Bolan set the wick for minimal illumination. In a fully darkened room, the lamp would cast its light around a radius of less than eighteen inches. But the dim illumination would be adequate to make his bull's-eye of adhesive tape stand out in stark relief against a darkened background.

Accuracy was the problem, sure.

Once the door was broken in, there would be seconds left to make the shot with a completely unfamiliar weapon. At his maximum efficiency, he might get off two rounds before the enemy responded with converging fire or kicked the lamp away and out of Bolan's range.

A moment, two at most, for the shot of a lifetime. If he screwed it up, with hostile guns inside the house....

"We're as ready as we'll ever be," he told the others. "Better take your places. Anything can hit us now, from here on in."

The four of them regrouped inside the parlor, moving toward their designated stations. Bolan crouched beside the farmer's padded easy chair, prepared to cover both the kitchen doorway and the parlor window. Jason Chadwick took position facing Bolan, at the far end of the parlor; from his place, the scattergun commanded doorways to both bedrooms and the lavatory. Over by the fireplace, with the sofa pulled around to offer shelter from incoming fire, the women huddled close together, keeping low and out of sight.

It was a shaky fortress, badly undermanned, but the warrior and his meager troops were out of time. Considering the limited resources, Bolan knew that they had done their best.

There was a human factor, yeah, where nerves and guts and heart came into play. One man or woman—grim, determined, motivated—could become an army in the proper cause.

Outside, a cloak of darkness settled across the landscape, turning fields of corn into a dark, amorphous mass outside the windows. By the barn, a light atop the wooden power pole was triggered by a photo cell, providing pale illumination for a portion of the barnyard.

Inside the darkened house, Mack Bolan and his little troop of conscripts settled down to wait.

THE COWBOY TOOK A FINAL DRAG on his cheroot and dropped the butt, ground it out beneath the heel of an expensive hand-tooled boot.

The hunter knew instinctively that it was time to move.

The gunners seemed to feel his tension, drifting toward him without any verbal summons. They formed a ring around him in the dusk, their muffled conversation dying down to whispers, finally stifled altogether.

"Time to start the ball," he told them all, unnecessarily. "I want a ring around the house, each man at his assigned position. Tommy, take a couple of guns and try to get inside the barn."

"It's done."

The Cowboy felt their hunger for the kill, knew that they were anxious to be off about their bloody business. They were up for this one, nerves strung tighter than piano wire by hours of waiting in the sun. Their collars might be limp with perspiration, but the men inside the crumpled suits were lean and mean, prepared for anything.

They were the best of their kind that blood money could buy, and the Cowboy would expect his money's worth tonight.

It was show time, right, and he was occupying center stage, with hungry eyes examining his every move. The men upstairs would judge him by his troops' performance, and if they let him down, the Cowboy would be burying his failures there, among the rows of corn.

"Stay on your toes," he told the ring of silent faces. "If anyone is planning to break out of there, they'll make a move tonight."

A general grumbling, with snickers interspersed. The sound reminded him of empty stomachs growling, jungle predators anticipating food. Raw meat, perhaps, still ripe with blood.

"I don't want any shooting at the house until I give the word," he said. "And use the silencers. A sound out here will carry twenty miles, and I don't want a flock of rubberneckers dropping by to watch a turkey shoot.''

A voice was raised beside him, on his left.

"Suppose they rabbit?"

"Anything that moves outside the house is bought and paid for."

"Goddamn right."

He looked around at them, demanding their attention by a force of will alone.

"I meant what I said about those silencers. I hear a gun out there tonight, it damn well better not be one of ours."

They were moving out in twos and threes, rustling through the darkened rows of corn to find their places on the firing line. He watched them go, his two lieutenants hanging back and waiting for instructions.

Out there in the darkness, the Cowboy knew his prey was waiting for him, every sense alert and nerves on edge. It would be nice if he could twist the knife and let them squirm before his men delivered the final killing stroke. A nervous enemy was often careless, made mistakes.

If he could get them going somehow, string them out and have them jumping at their own damn shadows, it would be a bonus.

And the inspiration struck him, suddenly.

"I want a landline to the house," he said.

"How's that?"

"A patch. We cut the line; I want it fixed again—just long enough to make a call. Can do?"

"Well. . . sure. Hell, yes, no problem."

"Fine. So do it."

Tall and solitary in the darkness, he could feel the old excitement rising in him now, the way it always did before a kill. A few more moments for his men to take position and everything would be in readiness.

The Cowboy smiled, his mirrored shades lending menace to the wolfish grimace on his face.

16

Waiting is a part of war, and darkness can be friend or foe, depending on the warrior's own experience and ability. For Bolan, it was neutral, a familiar state of being where he lived and fought as easily as in broad daylight. Easier, perhaps, if he was able to precipitate the battle, seize the initiative and follow through to victory. And he was used to waiting, right, in steamy Asian jungles, or the cluttered alleys of a major urban center. He had lain in wait for hours, days, to get a shot at some elusive enemy.

But he was used to playing the offensive team, accustomed by experience to waiting for a swift and sure assault. In Nam, and later—in his wars against the Mafia and urban terrorists—the game was hit and run, surprise the enemy and run him ragged, never resting. He had no time for digging trenches, fortifying outposts. Every stationary moment gave the enemy a chance to push ahead, trample the gentle civilizers underfoot.

Throughout his long crusade, the Executioner had opted for a lightning war, preferring always to initiate a strike rather than repelling one. In modern war, the first shot fired could be decisive, and it went against the Bolan grain to give up that advantage to the opposition. Still. . . .

Circumstances altered cases, dammit, in a battle zone. Tonight, the jungle fighter's options were severely limited—by his surroundings and his injuries, the shortage of supplies and able troops—and he would have to sacrifice that opening-gun advantage. Grudgingly, reluctantly, Mack Bolan was compelled to fight a grim defensive war.

And duty was a part of it, certainly, the sense of obligation that was keeping him inside the house and waiting for the opposition to arrive in force. He had delivered Jason Chadwick's family into peril, and he had to get them out of it again—or perish in the attempt.

He owed these people something, right. A helping hand. A chance. The possibility—however slim—of living through the terror that had followed him into their gentle lives.

Sergeant Mercy owed them that much. And the Executioner would make delivery on the obligation if he could.

For Jason and Emma.

Most especially for Toni.

The sudden jangling of the telephone was startling. Like the whirring of a dentist's drill, it seemed to bore inside the brain and find a pulsing nerve.

Toni Chadwick gasped, a frightened little sound, suppressed at once. The farmer cursed beneath his breath, and Bolan heard him shifting his position, making ready to repel surprise attackers, almost as if he was expecting them to enter through the trilling kitchen phone.

And it could only be the enemy, Mack Bolan knew. No believer in coincidence, the fighting man could not believe their sole communications link had not been deliberately severed, and now, for reasons still unclear, had been temporarily restored.

The soldier put his mind in overdrive, discarding possibilities as rapidly as they arose. No matter how he tried to think the angles through, he came up empty. There was simply no way anyone could harm them with the shrilling telephone. No chance of high-explosive charges planted in the earpiece, for example, and no serious risk of snipers if he took the natural precautions.

The phone was on its seventh ring when Bolan heard Emma Chadwick struggling to rise from her defensive crouch.

"Somebody better get that. Just in case."

"Stay down," the warrior told her gruffly. "I'll take it."

And he moved out, cautiously, maneuvering below the windowsill and snaking over the carpet. With the rifle probing out in front of him, he made the open doorway safely, slithered through and stood up beside the phone before its long eleventh ring was finished.

Bolan lifted the receiver, brought it to his ear. Momentary silence on the other end, the hollowness of a connection open, waiting. For an instant, he imagined he could feel a cold malevolence beyond the telephone receiver, concentrated Evil focused for the moment on his own destruction.

Softly, he addressed himself to silent Evil

"Yes?"

A windy hissing sound It took a moment for

Bolan to identify the mocking laughter, and he waited through it, holding on and swallowing his rage until it dwindled into nothingness. A neutral, monotonal voice addressed him.

"You're dead, hotshot."

Bolan waited.

"Trouble is, you're too damn dumb to know it."

Still he waited, and an edge was creeping into that voice. There was something underneath—surprise, perhaps, or anger—and the soldier knew that he had found a nerve. Bolan bit his tongue and kept the pressure on.

"Whatsa matter, asshole? Speechless?"

The enemy was reaching for sarcasm, but he stumbled over irritation, never got beyond it. And the Executioner was smiling now.

"Goddammit, boy, I'm coming after you. Tell the little woman there to keep it warm for papa."

Bolan chose his words deliberately and got it in before the vulture could continue.

"Don't bring anything you can't afford to lose," he said softly.

And he cradled the receiver.

He recognized the method, sure. The enemy was looking for a crack in the facade, attempting to insert a wedge and drive it home. The shrilling telephone could easily become a lethal weapon, if he let it.

Reaching out, the soldier looped his fingers through the cord where it connected with the wall and pulled. With a ripping sound, the cable separated from its moorings, and he left it dangling on the counter, taking up his rifle as he turned away.

At his back, the kitchen window detonated inward, spraying shattered glass across the dining table. Bolan recognized the angry hornet-hum of bullets streaming through the window, plowing into stove, refrigerator, cabinets.

In front of him, even as he hit a fighting crouch, the parlor window was imploding. Broken glass was everywhere, and once again the angry whine of incoming rounds was audible, immediately followed by the thudding into walls and furniture. Toni Chadwick screamed, a high, reflex sound of sudden panic.

They were using silencers, of course. The jungle fighter cursed beneath his breath and huddled against the kitchen counter, knees against his chest, waiting for the storm to pass. His little troop could weather this intact if everyone remained in place.

A cookie jar exploded opposite, and automatic fire was ripping unabated through the window above him. The holes were blossoming in walls and wooden cabinets, destroying cups and glasses, blasting bowls and plates to smithereens inside the cupboards.

Silencers.

There was something almost supernatural about the silent fusillade as it devoured furnishings and punctuated walls. Bolan heard the sound, dreamlike in the distance, of bedroom windows shattering into flying fragments.

You never hear the shot that kills you.

Bolan hit a prone position, snaked across the parlor carpet, crackling now with brittle shards. A foot above his head, the hostile fire was gouging furrows in the windowsill, releasing countless splinters.

He could hear the women sobbing, Jason's ragged, desperate cursing, and instinctively the warrior called to them above the sounds of battle.

"Stay down! They can't get at you if you keep your places!"

On the mantelpiece, an antique clock was dancing, skittering along beneath the driving force of rifle slugs. The TV erupted as bullets found the picture tube.

Bolan reached his corner, huddled in behind the cover of the easy chair. No time to worry now about the flimsy chicken wire withstanding so much concentrated fire. The screens would hold, or they would not. Right now, a more immediate concern was living through the fusillade—and keeping watch for the assault that must inevitably follow.

Heartbeats seemed to drag beneath the drumming leaden rain, and warrior Bolan saw the hurricane destruction of the living room progressing in a string of frozen, stop-action images. A magazine was lifted off the coffee table, pages fanning the air, and settled slowly to the littered floor. A vase was vaporized, the flowers standing upright for an instant, finally toppling into wilted disarray. A little cloud of mutilated stuffing hung above the sofa, artificial snowflakes sifting down, with bullets punching silent holes in their obscure formation.

The firing ended with the same dramatic suddenness that had marked its onslaught, as if someone had turned a tap to staunch the lethal flow. It left a vacuum, filled with ringing silence, in its wake.

Away to Bolan's left, beyond the open lavatory

door, the contents of a shattered medicine chest were trickling out and rattling in the sink. He scanned the devastation all around him, found the lantern with his eyes and let his pent-up breath escape, relieved to find the lamp upright and intact.

Bolan kept his voice down as he sounded off the roll call.

"Jason?"

"Yes."

"Mrs. Chadwick?"

"I'm all right."

"Toni?"

Momentary silence, then, "Okay."

His little troop of soldiers had survived the first offensive, right. The second, warrior Bolan realized, could not be far behind.

17

Crouching in the darkness, Bolan felt a sudden rush of déjà vu. He had been through it all before, and he could almost smell the jungle, hear exotic night cries through the shattered window on his right. The moment passed as swiftly as it had come, and he was back inside the farmhouse, waiting with his three draftees to meet an enemy that almost certainly had them outnumbered and outgunned.

The soldier's gut was telling him insistently that they would not have long to wait.

"Heads up!" he warned the others in a gruff stage whisper. "They'll be coming anytime now."

And, as if in answer to his words, a weight collided with the screen door of the porch, ripping through it noisily. The soldier heard their pointman fumbling with the latch, releasing it. The flimsy door banged open, rattling on its hinges.

Boot heels echoed on the porch, and Bolan held his breath, attempting to divine their numbers from the shifting, restless sounds. He made it three or four, at least, and now his night eyes could pick out the moving silhouettes in dim relief beyond the shattered kitchen window.

Bolan shifted slightly in his crouch, allowed the

.22's octagonal tube to rest across an arm of Jason's padded chair. If he was quick about it, he could bag a couple of them now, before they breached the inner line.

He shrugged the thought away. A killing shot was possible in theory, but Bolan knew the odds were stacked against him. With the little .22 he would require a mortal wound the first time out. If he should wing a target, even miss, he would have wasted precious ammunition and exposed himself to hostile fire for nothing.

It could wait until he had a chance to shave the odds a bit.

A heavy shoulder crashed against the kitchen door and found it firm; the human ram rebounded with a muffled curse. Another moment, and a boot heel struck the frame. Bolan heard something clatter onto the aging floorboards.

"Stupid jerk, you broke it!"

"Off my case, goddammit!"

"Off your ass. You got another doorknob in your pocket?"

"Can it, both of you. I've got a better way."

A solitary figure loomed before the broad expanse of window, stretching out a hand to tangle fingers in the chicken wire and pull it free.

"C'mon and help me clear this shit away."

The contact was explosive, searing. In a flash of incandescence Bolan saw the pointman, rigid fingers clenched on the screen and sparking, short hair standing up on end, his body stiff and quivering. Then the light evaporated in a burst of sparks.

But even in the dark, his man was on the line and frying. Bolan heard the crackle-hum of power flowing into flesh, the drumming heels. A nauseating new odor suddenly reminded him of napalmed bodies.

"Quick, get him offa there!"

Bolan caught another silhouette in profile, piston arms that rose and fell with something long and rigid in his hands. Something—broom or rifle butt—impacted on the withered fingers, jarring them free. The Executioner heard a heavy body strike the floor.

One less number, right, but it was slender satisfaction. They were still besieged.

The survivors had removed themselves from Bolan's field of vision now. He heard them moving, talking back and forth in nervous whispers. The sudden rush of static from a walkie-talkie overrode the other sounds. The advance men were in touch, for sure, and someone out there in the dark was giving orders.

Sounds of movement in the yard came from the direction of the barn. The troops were shifting—some of them, at any rate. Backlit by the light on the power pole, one of them cast a giant shadow on the parlor wall above the mantelpiece.

Bolan felt the sudden urge to take his shot and make the most of it while they were in the open, and again he let it slide away. He might have chanced it with a .30-.30, but the little .22 was short on knockdown power, and the moving targets made it too much of a gamble.

So he waited. They would have to come for him, and when they did—

An automatic weapon stuttered in the yard, a whisper audible despite the silencer, and then another joined the deadly chorus. Bolan ducked instinctively, but there were no incoming rounds; their target lay elsewhere.

With a crash of glass the barnyard light disintegrated, dropping a sudden cloak of darkness over house and barn. Severed at their junction by the bullets, power cables slithered down into the yard like dying serpents.

"We're open!" Bolan snapped. "Be ready!"

Even as he spoke, a radio was squawking on the Chadwick porch. At once a body struck the kitchen door, again; a muffled curse was lost as bullets started chewing up the doorframe. The lock was blown away, and strays were rattling around the kitchen, several of them reaching into the parlor.

In the final seconds left to him, the jungle fighter found his target, held the slender rifle steady on its padded rest. His index finger curled around the narrow trigger, and he found the hammer with his thumb, retracted it and locked it into readiness.

Another driving kick impacted on the kitchen door and drove it inward, slammed it back against the wall. A pair of hulking shapes were on the threshold, edging through with obvious reluctance. Even in the dark he saw that both of them were armed with stubby chatterguns, their muzzles lengthened, weighted by the silencers.

The two of them were his, and he could take them now. He *would* have taken them, if he had been a gambling man, but instead he kept his eye locked firmly on the white adhesive cross. His view was momentarily obstructed by a pair of tree-trunk legs, and then he had it back, the human secondary targets flanking his incendiary package. They were moving forward slowly.

Bolan stroked the trigger slightly, knew the shot was sour even as he worked the slide to prime another round. The matching muzzles of those deadly stutterguns were winking into life, the bullets coming high and working downward when he fired again.

The blasting cap and plastic charge erupted into heavy metal thunder, rattling the walls and ceiling overhead. A churning ball of flame enveloped Bolan's opposition, turned them into shrieking carbon-copy torches. Both of them discarded useless weapons as they blundered through a grisly dance of death.

Sergeant Mercy chose his moment, pumped a mercy round into the nearest dancer's face. The guy went down, and Bolan's .22 was tracking in a narrow arc, acquiring target number two an instant later. With the Winchester, recoil was nonexistent, but the spastic target spoiled his aim a fraction, and the tiny bullet burrowed into jawbone, knocking the gunner sprawling.

Bolan stood and crossed the twenty feet of open floor. The .22 pump in his right hand was balanced by the fire extinguisher he carried in his left.

The kitchen was a fiery shambles, with a dozen secondary flares ignited by the flying kerosene. Methodically, he hosed the bodies, then moved around, dousing fires. Ninety seconds saw it done, but the extinguisher was empty by the time he moved to crouch between the blackened bodies.

Number one was dead as hell, his face and body crisped, a drooling wound beneath an eye the evidence of Bolan's deadly marksmanship.

But number two was something else again. The guy was fried, all right, and Bolan's bullet had performed some sloppy orthodontics on the in-and-out, but he was hanging on to life with grim tenacity. The eyes, devoid of lids and lashes, fixed on Bolan's face; the swollen doughnut lips were moving soundlessly.

Bolan heard the silent plea, or else imagined it, and either way it was the same. He could not leave the guy this way, no more than he could waste a precious bullet to relieve his dying agony.

Without a moment's hesitation, Bolan set the rifle down and used both hands to raise the spent extinguisher above his head. The gunner saw it coming, turned his blistered face away, and Bolan drove the metal cylinder with all his strength against the hairless skull.

The tortured form went slack, relaxing into death. Bolan retrieved his .22 and scooped up the submachine guns before returning to his corner to check them over.

"Anybody hit?" he asked the empty air.

And one by one the negative responses reassured him, letting him know that—physically, at least—they all were still intact.

"Stay on your toes," he cautioned, whispering again. "We've mauled them, but it isn't over yet."

A murmur of assent, and he was already working

on the stutterguns, examining them both for load and damage. One of them was an Uzi with a folding stock, the other piece a squarish Ingram MAC-10.

Their magazines were incompatible, but the guns were thankfully both chambered in 9mm parabellum. Bullets taken out of one would fit the other if it came to that, and Bolan was encouraged by the uniformity of ammunition.

There was hope that he could capture other weapons, other ammo, make the enemy's artillery an instrument of his own destruction.

Bolan pulled the magazines and cursed beneath his breath. Between the two of them, he had eleven rounds, enough for one second of full-automatic fire from either weapon at the going cyclic rate.

And it was damn sure not enough to see them through.

He started calculating. If he loaded up the Uzi, with its capability of semiautomatic fire. . . .

Bolan emptied out the Ingram's magazine and started wedging cartridges into the Uzi's staggered box. He snapped the clip in place and primed the weapon, set the safety switch. Almost as an afterthought, he ditched the heavy silencer.

When they came in to get him, Bolan wanted fire and thunder on his side.

Tonight, for sure, he needed every edge available.

18

"They still don't answer."

"Damn."

The Cowboy keyed the walkie-talkie, held it close against his lips.

"All right, what's going on in there?"

"No way to tell. There was a flash, some kind of fire and then some shooting."

"A shotgun?"

"Negative. It sounded like a .22. No bigger than a .25, for sure."

So they were armed with something other than the scattergun in there. A .22, most likely, and he had to take for granted that the spearhead team had bungled, died in their initial attack. It followed that his quarry would be armed with automatic weapons now, and one of them, at least, knew how to use the military hardware.

It changed the equation dramatically, right, but the Cowboy was far from defeated. On the contrary it was time to push ahead full tilt.

The Cowboy had a feeling for his quarry now. He had received it on the telephone when he had called in to shake them up, a jarring revelation that had shaken him instead. Not the words alone; he had expected some defiance, a facade of courage in the face of certain death. It was the *tone* of voice, like an echo from the tomb.

A stone-cold killer's voice, for sure. The Cowboy knew it well enough; the voice was not unlike his own.

And the warnings handed down by his superiors had greater meaning for him now. Forget about the farmer, anybody else inside the house. His troops were up against a true professional, and he had taken out a pair of them—no, make it *five*—already. No concessions could be won from such a man, and they would have to blast him out of there, remove him from the smoking ashes piece by piece if necessary.

It would take a full assault to rout him, and every moment wasted gave the enemy an opportunity to strengthen his defenses.

The Cowboy raised the radio and keyed the mike.

"Roll in Team B," he snapped, "and have that backup ready if we need it."

Momentary hesitation as the order was digested by his pointman in the darkness.

"Roger that."

The hunter let the walkie-talkie drop and leaned against the Lincoln's dusty fender. Half a mile away, across the darkened field, his troops were in position, primed and ready to assault the farmhouse for a second time. Their lives—*his* life—was riding on the fate of that assault. And if it fell apart....

He had the backup team, prepared to plug the gaps as they appeared. If worse should come to worst, the Cowboy would step in and take a hand himself. If necessary.

Suddenly, he hoped that would not be necessary.

Something in the distant, disembodied voice had put him off, disturbed him in a way that nothing had for years. The Cowboy could not deny it.

It was fear.

The faceless stranger had inspired a feeling in the Cowboy he could not admit to anyone. Not even to himself.

The Cowboy was afraid, so be it. Standing in the silent darkness now, he recognized the only antidote for that unwelcome feeling. He would have to face the object of his fear and kill it personally, wash away the stain of cowardice with blood. There was no other way to pin it down.

BOLAN HEARD THEM coming through the silent darkness. He began to prepare himself before they hit the house on all four sides at once. A charging gunner hit the parlor window screen and burst through, entangled in the chicken wire and cursing as he tumbled to the floor. The guy was scrambling to his feet and milking little probing bursts out of his silenced Uzi as he tried to get his bearings, pumping parabellum rounds into the walls and ceiling.

Bolan tracked the lurching target with his .22 and stroked the trigger lightly, holding steady as the little stinger ripped through flesh and gristle. It elicited a howl of pain, but his assailant still was up and moving, searching for a target with his blazing stuttergun.

Bolan pumped the rifle's slide, ejecting empty brass and chambering another round. A hesitation to correct, regaining target acquisition, and his sights were framed inside the yawning oval of the gunner's lips when he squeezed off a second time. Forty grains of screaming death impacted on the target's pharynx, burrowed through and shattered into fragments at the junction of his skull and vertebrae. Instantly deprived of motor functions as his spine was severed, Bolan's mark melted backward in the clumsy sprawl of death.

And they were all around Bolan now. A pair of automatic weapons opened up inside the kitchen, driving him down and under cover. Above the whisper of the silenced man-shredders, he could hear the other shock troops battering their way through undefended bedroom windows.

Bolan wriggled back behind the padded easy chair, and it was taking hits, the stuffing sagging from a dozen jagged rents in the upholstery. They had found the range, and they could blast him out of there if Bolan sat around and waited for it.

Counting down the numbers now, he switched the slender rifle to his left hand, gripped the Uzi with his right and set the fire selector switch on automatic mode. A single stroke would empty his slim reserve of parabellum ammunition in a searing stream.

The Executioner was cornered, right. Pinned down. Another moment under fire would be his last.

And in the circumstances, Bolan planned to take the only option open to him.

He was blasting out.

If it was time to die, the soldier chose to meet his moment standing up, with all guns blazing. Carrying the fire to his opponents, yeah.

The warrior coiled his legs beneath him, braced himself to spring. The hammer of his pulse was deafening; it drowned the ripping noise of bullets shredding fabric inches from his head. Another instant, and the numbers all ran down to zero.

Then Bolan made his move.

FOR A FROZEN MOMENT, Jason Chadwick was surrounded by the steamy jungle once again, waiting for the enemy to rush his muddy foxhole. It was 1943, and he was back in Bougainville, prepared to kill or die. Except the Japanese had always come with shrieks and howls and whistles blowing; these new enemies were silent, swift and sure.

He was ready when a human form exploded through the parlor window, ripping down the screen with its momentum. Jason swung his scattergun to meet the threat, and then he saw the darting tongue of flame from Frank LaMancha's .22. The intruder was returning fire, but awkwardly, encumbered by the twisted chicken wire and staggered by the bullets ripping into him. He stumbled, sprawling, and—

Crashing, thrashing noises from the nearest bedroom suddenly demanded his attention. Someone—more than one invader, by the sound of it—had breached their slim defenses on another side.

They were surrounded, dammit, and the time to do or die was now.

The farmer raised the shotgun, snugged the butt against his shoulder and aligned the sights on the dark rectangle of the open bedroom doorway.

A hulking body filled the portal, swiftly stepped

into the living room. The automatic weapon in his hands was obvious, despite the darkness, bulky muzzle searching for a target.

Jason looped his finger tight around the shotgun's single trigger, squeezing. As if alerted to the danger the intruder twisted, dropping to a combat crouch instinctively. It was enough to spoil the farmer's perfect shot, but not enough for the invader to save himself completely.

Jason's weapon roared and bucked against his shoulder. At a range of less than twenty feet, the charge of shot had little opportunity to spread before it struck the gunman's shoulder, spinning him around in a horrendous spray of blood and mutilated flesh. The stunning impact threw him backward, tumbling across the sofa, out of sight.

A second human shape was piling through the doorway now, already crouching and alert to peril from the darkness. Jason took a moment to correct his aim, and it was all he had before the mercenary spotted him and swung his submachine gun deftly onto target.

Their weapons opened up in unison, and Jason had a split-second glimpse of winking muzzle-flame before the shotgun's recoil blurred his vision. For an instant he imagined he could see the pellets strike their target. Then a parabellum shocker struck Jason's weapon, knocked it spinning from his grasp.

A fragment of the shattered bullet opened up his cheek beneath one eye, and he was driven backward, shoulders banging hard against the wall with force that took his breath away. The world was reeling, and Jason knew he was falling just before his skull impacted on the upright heater to his left.

The flash of light behind his eyes was blinding, and the darkness swallowed him alive.

HUDDLED BEHIND THE SOFA, Toni Chadwick tried to blot the sounds of mortal combat from her mind. Beside her, Emma sat trembling against the wall, with knees drawn up against her chest and both hands covering her ears.

Toni's heart went out to Emma, but her mind was firmly fixed on survival. In her lap, she clutched a wicked ten-inch carving knife selected from the meager kitchen arsenal; a second blade, together with the cleaver, lay between the women on the floor. And if the battle went against them, as it almost surely would, the flimsy arms would have to do.

She heard the ripping sound as screen and nails were separated at the parlor window. The muffled stutter of an automatic weapon, punctuated by the high, falsetto yapping of a little .22. And now, the crashing sounds of violent entry seemed to come from everywhere at once, smothering her. They were separated from her only by a flimsy wall, the open bedroom door.

The lady felt a presence close by, then the world exploded overhead. With ringing ears, she recognized the roar of Jason's scattergun. A bloody mist was falling, shreds of fabric interspersed with something else, and Toni's mind rebelled. She felt herself about to vomit.

A tumbling body struck the couch and toppled

over, slithered down headfirst across the ruined cushions. Toni lost her balance, caught herself without relinquishing her grip on the knife and spun around to face the threat.

A man was sprawled across the couch, head down, suspended by his knees. Even in the darkness, Toni saw his arm was missing. No—it was attached, but dangling out of joint and clinging to its socket by a single, twisted strand of flesh. His blood was everywhere.

But this one was alive.

His eyes were open, staring back at Toni with a kind of glazed expression.

The gunman's coat had fallen open, revealing an automatic pistol in its rigging. As Toni watched, the dying man was groping for it, trying desperately to reach the holstered weapon.

And he was getting there, by inches. Under all the pain, there was a stark, triumphant grimace on his face.

Toni had to act, and swiftly. If he reached the pistol....

She was on her knees beside him in a single fluid movement, both hands locked around the wooden handle of her carving knife. A final moment's hesitation as the bright steel flickered overhead, and then she brought it down, astonished as the razor tip disappeared from sight. She put her weight behind it, and the blade was grating, shuddering against his ribs, setting Toni's teeth on edge.

The gunner stiffened, writhing and growling at her like a wounded animal. The lady lost her balance but retained her grip; the blade snapped off an inch below the hilt, remaining in the body.

Her assailant convulsed, no longer trying for the pistol now. His single hand was clutching at her, fingers tangling in the folds of Toni's woolen shirt before she had a chance to slip away.

The one-armed mercenary clung to her tenaciously, his weight an anchor dragging Toni down. A final lunge that popped the buttons on her shirt, and Toni reached the cleaver, brought it up, around and down without attempting to select a target. Frantically she hacked away, aware that she was covered now with blood: it fouled her hair and clothing, smeared her face and trickled down the valley of her breasts, made fingers slippery on the cleaver's grip.

She had a vague awareness of the clutching fingers loosening their hold, relaxing. With a final manic blow, she left the cleaver firmly planted in its target.

And now revulsion dominated panic. Toni uttered a silent plea for merciful oblivion, but there was no release for Frank LaMancha's lady soldier. There was nothing now except the hammering of guns.

19

Bolan's lunge propelled him over and across the riddled easy chair. He landed on the floor beyond it in a diving shoulder roll. Two kitchen gunners tracked him closely, but his move had taken them off guard, allowed the Executioner a slight margin for his desperate play.

From a prone position, Bolan swung his captured Uzi around. His targets were the winking muzzle-blasts of hostile guns. Hungry parabellum rounds were searching for him, drilling through the wall a foot above his head and to his right.

Bolan squeezed the trigger, held it down and emptied the Uzi in rapid fire, a single vicious figure eight that swept them both away. He had a fleeting glimpse of bodies reeling backward, weapons pumping fire wildly into the ceiling, bringing down a rain of plaster.

Bolan's ears were ringing from the burst of automatic fire, the double-thumping blast of Jason's 12-gauge, when the sound of running feet intruded on his racing thoughts.

Before he could react, a gunner cleared the bedroom doorway at his back and stumbled over Bolan's outstretched legs. The trooper lost his balance, reeling, going down. Reacting swiftly, Bolan jabbed the muzzle of his little .22 beneath the gunner's chin and pulled the trigger.

The explosion, muffled and confined at skin-touch range, propelled his human target backward into free-fall, spewing blood from an ugly hole beneath his jawline. The man tumbled back across the easy chair, bits of bone and brain adhering to the cushion where his shattered skull had come to rest.

Bolan was on his feet before another gunner showed himself, closing fast. No time to chamber up another round as Bolan pivoted to meet the rush, reacting with the instinct of a jungle predator. Instead of backing off, he moved to meet his enemy halfway, the rifle whipping up and over on a sharp collision course with that charging face.

A numbing jolt as walnut stock met flesh and bone; they shattered simultaneously, Bolan's rifle stock a flying piece of shrapnel in the darkness. The mercenary stumbled through an awkward little pirouette, both hands uplifted to defend his mangled face.

The jungle fighter followed up his slim advantage, swung the rifle onto line and pumped a rapid triple punch between the bloody fingers of his adversary's hands, the little stingers ripping into nose and cheeks at point-blank range. The dying gunner melted back, his substance soaking through the bedroom carpet.

A sudden deathly stillness settled across the indoor hellzone, and Bolan took a moment to pick out the muffled sounds of sobbing from behind the couch. At least someone was still alive back there, but for the moment that person would have to wait. He scanned the killground, assured himself that all their enemies were down and out of action.

For the moment, right.

They had repelled a second rush, but they were far from out of danger. He did a rapid body count. Make it ten so far. And how damn many left to go, just waiting in the outer darkness for a signal to attack?

A cautious soldier never underestimated opposition strengths. He took the worst for granted. And waited.

Bolan was a cautious soldier, sure, but he did not possess the luxury of time. His little troop was cornered, with their backs against the wall, and their success in the initial holding actions gave him little satisfaction.

He made another scan, this time for friendly casualties, and settled on the crumpled form of Jason Chadwick. In a flash, the soldier was beside him, checking for wounds. There was a ragged gash below one eye, a lump behind his ear, but the older man was otherwise unhurt, already struggling up to consciousness as Bolan felt the women close beside him. They were crowding in to help as he maneuvered Jason upright, held him there until the farmer could support himself.

"Are you all right?"

"I'm fine—just hit my head is all." The farmer touched his bloody cheek with cautious fingers. "Give me time to catch my breath."

He was staring at the younger woman now, a blank expression on his face, and Bolan followed Jason's eye, focusing on Toni for the first time since their desperate battle started.

In the moonlight filtering through a window, she was like a vision out of hell. The auburn hair was tangled, matted, and the tracks of tears were stark against her bloody cheeks, but he knew instinctively the blood was not her own.

A glance across her shoulder, and he spied a lifeless gunner draped across the couch, head down, the cleaver buried in his ravaged throat.

The lady had been taking care of business, and Mack Bolan knew the symptoms of impending shock. He had seen enough of it on other youthful faces in the aftermath of combat. It was Toni's blood initiation, and the shock could push her either way.

The warrior slipped an arm around her shoulders, held her close and began to whisper, "Hold it all together, Toni. You're a natural survivor, and there's nothing wrong with that. Live large."

A shudder gripped her, and she half turned to press herself against him now, no longer holding back the tears. Bolan held her for a moment, counting down the numbers, painfully aware that they were running out of time.

"We haven't got a lot of time," he told them all. "We need to strip the bodies down for arms and ammunition, get ready for the next wave."

Jason Chadwick cleared his throat.

"How many do you think there are?"

Bolan shrugged.

"Impossible to say. We've hurt them, but we can't take anything for granted. Anyway, we've got a better chance now than we had an hour ago."

And as he spoke, the Executioner wondered to himself if that was true. If hardware made the crucial difference in the long run.

He was moving toward the nearest body, keeping low, when Toni's voice arrested him.

"What *is* that? Do you smell it?"

And he did. A smell of burning, subtly different than the acrid stench of gunsmoke, faint at first but growing stronger. The odor seemed to come from nowhere, and from everywhere at once.

"The cellar!"

That from Emma, and the soldier found her kneeling with her back to him, a finger pointing in the direction of the bathroom door. Bolan strained his eyes, saw a thread of smoke curling upward through a hairline crack between the floorboards. The slender wisp was followed moments later by another. And another

"What's down there?"

Emma answered him.

"It's storage, mostly. Some preserves. Storm windows."

"The stairs."

"Outside. Against the kitchen wall, east side."

"All right. I'll have to chance it."

As he spoke, they heard a motor sputtering to life and revving up above them. In an instant, it was followed by a whining, ripping sound.

"Chain saw!" Jason snapped. "They're cutting through."

And they were out of time, for sure. All the numbers whittled down to zero.

"Arm yourselves," he cautioned. "From the time I leave, you're in a free-fire zone. Kill anything that moves."

Bolan scuttled across the living room, homing on his little cache behind the armchair. On the way, he snared an Ingram, loaded to capacity. Another moment, and he had the sack containing his homemade grenades. Behind him, Toni and her in-laws had begun to forage gingerly among the scattered corpses, hefting automatic weapons, stripping pistols out of shoulder holsters.

They would have to stand without him, on their own.

His biggest problem now was getting outside. Alive.

They would have spotters posted, certainly, but he was hoping that initial losses might have sapped their strength and opened up some holes along the firing line. A moment would suffice, a watcher off his station, or distracted long enough for Bolan to effect his exit from the farmhouse.

And a window would do nicely for his purposes, if he could just select one that was unobserved. It was a chancy game, attempting to invade the hostile mind and second-guess an adversary, but the Executioner was left with little choice.

Correction. There was no damn choice at all.

If he sat still, all four of them were dead. The opposition would not risk another costly rush if they could torch the house or drop a satchel charge from overhead. Whichever way they chose to play it, Bolan and his little troop were literally sitting on a time bomb.

He decided on the bedroom. A casual sentry would expect evacuees to use the kitchen door and porch, perhaps the spacious parlor window, as an exit. Smaller bedroom windows were inferior escape routes, and with any luck at all would be assigned second priority.

If they had thinned the opposition out sufficiently.

If nerves and sheer attrition had combined to make the mercenaries careless.

If.

And if he was mistaken in his calculations. . . .

The Executioner severed the morbid train of thought before it had a chance to carry him away. Defeatism was a sickness, terminal variety. A soldier who surrendered to it might as well confront his enemy unarmed. But Bolan was fighting back with everything he had, until the final spark of life was smothered in the darkness.

It was cool and dark inside the master bedroom, and he stepped across a mercenary felled by Jason's shotgun. Stooping briefly, he retrieved a Colt Commander from the lifeless gunner's shoulder rigging, wedged it inside the waistband of his overalls.

He crouched beside the open window frame, his jungle senses probing the night. A velvet breeze caressed his face, inviting him outside to join the dance.

It was an offer he could not refuse.

Without a backward glance, Mack Bolan wriggled through the window, merging with the outer darkness, and was gone.

20

Soft grass cushioned Bolan's landing below the window. He froze in combat crouch, immobile, but his every sense was on alert, waiting for a shout of warning or a muffled fusillade from the perimeter. When neither came, he let his breath escape from aching lungs. He moved away from there, the captured Ingram up and ready, taking extra care with the weighted sack.

Out here, the revving of the saw was amplified, redoubled, filling up the night and grating on the warrior's nerves. He let it pass for now and circled to his left, intent upon the cellar. At the moment, smoke and fire were greater dangers than the gunner on the roof, and Bolan had to rout the infiltrator before the enemy brought the house down in flames.

Another moment, and he reached the target unopposed. The slanting double doors were open wide, thrown back on either side; below him, sturdy wooden steps descended into darkness. Tattered wisps of smoke were rising through the open hatchway, thicker now than it had been inside the house. The fire was taking hold down there and growing. He could hear it now, a crackling like a sheet of cellophane in palsied hands.

Time to move, and there was nowhere for the Executioner to go but down.

He crouched beside the bag and opened it, withdrew a makeshift hand grenade. A pair of woolen socks was rolled down around the lip of the explosive can, to help protect the blasting cap, and now he peeled them off, discarded them and straightened up, returning to the open cellar door.

Beneath his feet, a human shape was stirring in the smoky darkness, closing on the stairs. Bolan held the can at full arm's length, the blasting cap inverted, and released it. He was backpedaling away from there, when the crude grenade erupted into hollow thunder. A cloud of smoke and dust rolled up and out from underground, and jagged shrapnel set the wooden doors to flapping.

Bolan followed with a rush, the Ingram leading as he took the battered stairs in stride. A crumpled body waited for him at the bottom of the stairs, spread with one leg twisted underneath him. He had worn a gas mask to protect him from the smoke, but it had not deflected roofing nails from ripping through his throat and chest and abdomen. The guy was far beyond resisting, and the Executioner dismissed him, moving on to find and fight the fire that he had kindled in his final moments.

In a corner of the basement, jagged teeth of flames were rising from a pile of old magazines, already nibbling at adjacent wooden shelving. Bolan cast about for something to fight the blaze. He settled on a dusty patchwork quilt he found atop a hope chest.

He waded in, the flying quilt a bludgeon that he

used to beat and smother out the licking flames. Gagging on the acrid smoke, he held his ground and fought it out until the fire had been reduced to embers, and the embers scattered wide. He poked among the magazines and ground them underfoot until he finally satisfied himself the fire was out.

Above him, Bolan's little troop was out of danger—for that moment.

There was no way to secure the cellar with the time and tools at hand. His enemies could try again if Bolan let them have the opportunity, but he had other plans in mind.

The Executioner was launching an offensive of his own this time, reverting to a style of warfare that had served him well in other killgrounds.

Moving cautiously, he followed the ascending smoke as it evacuated, reemerging into cool, clean darkness topside. No one was responding to the blast of his grenade, and Bolan offered up a silent prayer of thanks. The hostiles must be getting careless; they had either failed to hear the detonation, or dismissed it as a natural result of fire raging in the cellar. Either way, it gave the jungle fighter a bit of breathing room.

Bolan circled back, retracing his steps and avoiding the front of the house with its clear field of fire toward the barn. If they were thin enough in numbers now, the enemy would concentrate on that approach, commanding all the major exits.

Navigating by ear, he reached a point at which the whining, snarling saw was loudest. Deprived of visual contact with his target, Bolan had to guess the position as he stooped, withdrew another high-explosive can from his sack and stripped the stocking cap away.

The warrior knew that any small mistake or fluke could spoil his shot. If the can did not impact upon its blasting cap, or if the cap should fail to detonate for any reason, it would skitter off harmlessly across the sloping shingles.

He shrugged away the momentary hesitation, then let fly the weighted can of high explosives. It looped away and out of sight as Bolan counted down the seconds to doomsday or failure.

Overhead, a flash of brilliant light, the crack of an explosion, and the farmhouse shuddered from the blast. A strangled scream, and then the growling saw was airborne, spinning in a cloud of exhaust smoke before it plunged to earth and died almost at Bolan's feet. Above him, desperate scuffling noises, then the barrel-rolling sound of a descending body—tumbling *away* from Bolan.

And his mark had fallen down the opposite slope—in the direction of the porch and barnyard.

With his captured Ingram up and ready, Bolan doubled back, aware of the impending danger, knowing he could not avoid it. The warrior was exposed, and now his only hope of a successful follow-through would be to make it brisk and bold. Take it to the enemy and ram it down their throats before they had a chance to organize effective counter-measures.

It was down to Bolan's kind of war, against the odds The kind of one-man war he had been fighting, more or less, since his return from Vietnam. A dozen automatic weapons might be waiting for him in the barn or the surrounding fields, but Bolan owed the effort to his three reluctant allies. To himself, damn right.

And allies—volunteer or otherwise—were more than simply soldiers in a common cause. They were complications, and sometimes fatal ones at that. In his soul, the warrior was responsible for each and every one of them. When they blew it, when *he* failed them, Bolan bore the scars of loss alone.

His mind, unbidden, started running down the roster, men and women who had sacrificed their all in Bolan's holy war. He shut off the gloomy train of thought. The dead had made their sacrifice already; Bolan's war tonight was for the living.

He was closing quickly on the northwest corner of the house, prepared for anything except the bloody scarecrow that appeared directly in his path, approaching on a hard collision course. The specter seemed disoriented, following the wall with arms outstretched, and Bolan saw at once that he was blind.

It was the rooftop gunner, battered but alive. Even in the darkness, Bolan could pick out the ragged wounds where flying nails had pulped his eyes and sliced a bloody channel right across his nose. The heads of other roofing nails protruded from his cheeks and jaw.

Bolan moved to intercept the lurching zombie, swung his Ingram hard against the mutilated skull. The gunner stumbled, fell, and Bolan followed him, a silent, stalking jungle predator. The enemy was on his back and struggling feebly to rise when Bolan drove a crushing heel against his larynx, brought an end to pain.

That made it twelve. A butcher's dozen, yeah.

How many more would have to die before the nightmare ended?

Bolan edged around a corner of the porch, and suddenly he did not need to look for anyone or anything. The enemy found *him*, announcing the discovery with a near-miss burst that shredded screen above his head. The second burst was right on target—but Bolan had retreated out of range.

Now, with time to think, the soldier knew exactly what he had to do in order to survive. Pinpoint the gunners. Take a measure of their strength, dispersal, weaponry if possible. Neutralize the threat with swift, effective counteraction.

All of which required the jungle fighter to expose himself again, in order to assess the hostile force. It was a split-second operation that could feel like a lifetime.

Or end one.

Timing was the key—reflexes coupled with visual acuity. If Bolan could not spot his targets first time out, he might not have a second chance.

The warrior poked his head around the corner, scanning rapidly with narrowed eyes. He was ready, waiting, when an automatic rifle opened up, this muzzle-flash distinctive even with the silencer attached. He ducked and scuttled backward, flattening himself against the wooden planking as a swarm of tumblers sought him out.

A single gunner. In the hayloft of the barn.

It made his problem marginally smaller—if the gunner was, in fact, alone. Assuming that he did not have backup staked out and waiting for the fox to make his move.

Bolan launched himself headlong from cover, somersaulting out of shadow into his assailant's line of fire. The movement ended with him in a fighting crouch and facing toward the darkened barn, his weapon braced and ready.

Startled, his assailant took a second to react, and Bolan had his answer ready when the hostile weapons stuttered to life. He pressed the Ingram's trigger, held it down and swung the stubby muzzle in a roaring arc. The steel-jackets rattled out at seven hundred rounds a minute as he hosed the open loading bay from left to right and back again.

The assault rifle tracked him, homing onto target, and he heard the bullets whispering around him, eating up the ground in front of him and to either side. Another moment and the creeping rounds would find him, or the Ingram would exhaust its load—and either way, the end result would be identical.

The final number clicked, his little stuttergun gave a dying burst—and nothing.

No incoming rounds.

Out of darkness, Bolan saw a slouching figure as it suddenly appeared and teetered on the verge of falling. The sniper's empty rifle tumbled from his dying fingers, clattered in the yard below. His life was running out through half a dozen holes, and in another moment he plunged headlong through the opening, a lifeless, sprawling bundle.

Bolan straightened up, the smoking submachine gun dangling uselessly at his side. He waited, half expecting other weapons to explode around him, other rounds to seek him out and knock him reeling into death and darkness everlasting.

He did not expect the sudden glare of headlights, kicking into high beams, blinding Bolan as a Caddy crew wagon lumbered toward him out of nowhere, flattening the stalks of corn like so much tender grass before a reaper. Grim Reaper, right, and now the brilliant orbs were carving tunnels through the night, transfixing Bolan where he stood and pinning him at center stage.

21

The Cowboy crouched in darkness, staring at the farmhouse through his mirrored shades. The stainless-steel Smith & Wesson .44 was heavy in his fist, but it helped restore his failing confidence. It made him strong.

And inner strength was nearly all that he had left.

He had put two waves of men inside the house, ten sharp guns in all, and none of them were ever coming out again. His backup team was shot to hell, and now the sound of firing from the yard informed him that his target was alive and kicking ass.

Okay, it's come down to this.

The Cowboy moved out from the corn, gliding across the open stretch of ground. He reached the bedroom window unobserved and knelt before it for a moment, listening, before he slipped inside.

He required a moment to adjust his eyes, and briefly contemplated taking off the shades, but finally dismissed the thought. Somehow, the mirrored glasses made him feel invulnerable.

He crossed the littered room, avoiding shattered glass and toppled furniture. And he knew that he was all alone inside the bedroom, but out there, beyond the open door, he smelled his prey, their fear and trembling.

The Cowboy did not plan to keep them waiting long.

One of his professionals was lying lifeless in the doorway. He resisted a sudden impulse to lash out and grind a boot heel in the shredded face. His business here was with the living—and with those about to die.

Someone would be waiting just beyond the open door, no doubt about it.

With all the wasted soldiers he had put in here, the hicks would have a smorgasbord of weapons to select from, assuming that they had the smarts to use them. Even if they lacked the skill, an idiot could have a lucky day, and parabellum bullets had no way of telling friend from foe.

It was the Cowboy's job to take the guesswork out of it, make doubly sure that any luck his adversaries had was bad.

Standing just inside the bedroom door, he hesitated, easing back the hammer of his stainless-steel Smith & Wesson. From his belt, the mercenary drew a smoke grenade the size of a beer can, hefted it.

He looped a finger through the safety ring and yanked it free, already winding up an underhand release before the can began to spark and sputter. Almost absentmindedly, he watched it bounce across the living room, releasing clouds of artificial fog to camouflage his entrance.

Low and fast, he took the doorway in a rush, the Smith & Wesson sweeping ahead of him and seeking targets. He was ready for it when a submachine gun opened up to his left, discharging half a magazine in one indignant burst.

The Cowboy pivoted, and at a range of less than thirty feet there was no need to aim. The silver Magnum was a ravenous extension of himself as he swiveled into target acquisition.

A single round was all it took, 240 grains of sudden death directly through his target.

JASON CHADWICK HEARD SOMETHING land on the living-room floor, followed by the sound of rapid boot heels on the boards. Swinging his sights on the intruder, the farmer triggered the unfamiliar SMG. He tried to ride the recoil of the captured weapon, but bone-deep weariness conspired with gagging smoke to spoil his aim. The little chattergun was climbing hopelessly before a dozen rounds had left the muzzle, chewing up the ceiling and very little else.

A tremendous roar filled the room and something very like a cannonball slammed into his shoulder. Weakened fingers lost their grip on his gun and he felt himself being propelled through space. A solid barrier arrested his flight and several colors swam before his eyes, the myriad hues changing to black as nothing seemed to make sense anymore.

THE KILLER STRAIGHTENED UP, searching for another mark. The target came to him, colliding with him in the smoky darkness. Smaller than the gunman he had blown away, this one was a lightweight. The Cowboy turned to meet his enemy, the barrel of his Smith &

Wesson chopping down on a wrist and emptying the hand of weaponry. He followed through, a stunning backhand to the face, got one arm looped around his victim, who was spinning from the blow.

His hand closed around a firm breast.

The Cowboy had a sudden inspiration, even as he pressed the muzzle of his weapon up against the lady's cheek and held it there.

She was his ticket out, a passport to success when he was staring brutal failure in the face. She changed the whole percentage.

The Cowboy was a sterling judge of character. He knew his enemy, though he had never met the man or even seen his face. He could predict how this one would react to damsels in distress, and it was all the lead he needed.

While the poor, pathetic bastard was deciding how to save her ass, the Cowboy would be busy blowing them away. The gunner first, and then the broad. It would be too easy.

BOLAN STUMBLED as he reached the corner, and that saved his life. A burst of tumblers razored the air above his head exactly where his shoulder blades had been a moment earlier. Then he was away and out of there, scrambling along on hands and knees. He gained the sanctuary of the corner and slid around it, welcoming the momentary shelter.

Forty yards away and closing rapidly, the juggernaut was bearing down on him, the flankers keeping pace and wisely saving ammunition now until a target was presented. In another moment they would have him, bring the lights and guns to bear.

Bolan ripped the satchel wide open, stripped his final crude grenade of its protective covering. Bolan moved, and not away this time, but toward the enemy. His trackers would have planned for everything—except a suicidal rush directly down their throats. With any luck at all, initial shock would get him into range, and guts would do the rest.

He cleared the corner running, one arm cocked, prepared to lob the high-explosive can with deadly accuracy. He chose the Caddy's windshield as his target and let fly, already veering, rolling to his left and digging for the Colt Commander as the riflemen began to snipe at him.

The Executioner was prone and trying desperately to wriggle out of range when the plastique erupted into oily flame, devouring the Cadillac and anyone inside. The shock wave flattened infantry on either side, and Bolan held his belly-down position as a swarm of twisted roofing nails whined overhead. Another moment, and the crew wagon's fuel tank followed in a ringing secondary blast, the dinosaur settling on melted tires, hissing in the throes of fiery death.

Bolan made it to his feet, the autoloader in his fist and ready as he crossed the firelit yard. To the left, one of his pursuers was attempting to prevent himself from frying, using blistered hands to slap at flames devouring his trousers. Bolan braced the heavy .45 with both hands and put a single deadly bullet through the screaming face.

The Executioner found the second, final gunman struggling to his feet and searching all around him for the rifle he had dropped. It was a toss-up whether he discovered it or Bolan first, but his reaction was immediate. A diving lunge, with arms outstretched and fingers splayed to grasp the silenced M-16, a look of desperation on his bloodied face.

And Bolan helped him get there, popping off a rapid double punch that flipped his target over in midair and laid him out on his back.

Alone among the dead, Mack Bolan straightened from his fighting crouch and let the pistol slip a few degrees off target. His wound had opened up again, and he could feel the blood soaking through his shirt and trickling down inside his overalls.

Make it sixteen down, and Bolan wondered if at last he might have swept the field. Even as the question was materializing, his answer kicked the screen door open and ambled down the wooden steps.

A lanky gunner, dressed in Western garb, with Toni Chadwick clasped in front of him to form a living shield. The muzzle of a stainless-steel revolver was pressed against her skull, the pistolero's other arm around her chest. The enemy was smiling at him now, reminding Bolan of a hungry reptile, eyes invisible behind some kind of mirrored glasses.

TONI CHADWICK GRIMACED with agony.

The fingers locked around her breast were talons, totally devoid of sexuality, an instrument of pain.

Her captor jammed the muzzle of his handgun up against her cheek with brutal force. The polished steel was warm from recent firing, and it stank of powder smoke. A sudden image of the bullet striking Jason turned her stomach.

When he whispered in her ear, the gunman's voice

was coarse and hollow, like a night wind among the headstones of a cemetery.

"You and me are going for a little walk," he snarled. "Do exactly what I tell you, when I tell you, and you just might keep on breathing. Understand?"

She nodded, already taking stock of her condition and the chances of escape. Toni had a fair idea of what her captor had in mind, and she determined on the spot to die, provoke him into shooting her, before she let him use her to destroy LaMancha.

The gunman started moving, pushing her ahead of him. He had released her breast, the strong arm circling her waist and keeping her from making any sudden moves.

They were crossing the burned-out ruin of the kitchen when a powerful explosion rocked the house, produced a sudden gust of wind that set the screen door flapping on the porch. An instant later, there was yet another blast, and she could see the leaping flames outside, consuming what appeared to be a vehicle.

The gunman froze, and she could feel his tension as a rapid string of gunshots followed the explosions. She realized the weapon was unsilenced, and the implication gave her sudden hope. If Frank LaMancha was alive and armed out there....

Her captor hesitated for a moment, then propelled her toward the door, as if he had arrived at some decision.

Toni's foot made contact with the outstretched fingers of a burned and battered corpse. She felt the nausea rising, threatening to overcome her, but the gunner at her back responded with a violent shake that snapped her out of it, returned her from the brink of madness to a tenuous grip on sanity.

She had to keep her wits about her. An alertness, the ability to think, to plan, to *act*, was all that stood between her and sudden death. Her own alertness might, in fact, be all the hope that Frank LaMancha had, as well.

They reached the porch, no longer dark or cool now in its close proximity to the fire. The lady had a moment left before they reached the doorway proper, and she looked the burning Caddy over briefly, sickened by the grisly, slouching scarecrow wedged behind the steering wheel. She tore her eyes away from there and scanned the yard, the other twisted bodies—until she found LaMancha.

He was standing tall, almost princely in the firelight, watching as they made the steps, negotiated them, and moved away toward open ground. The gunman kept his arm around Toni, holding her against him like a shield.

"'Gratulations, Slick." The graveyard voice was mocking. "You got 'em all, except for one."

LaMancha was looking past her, at the gunman's face.

"Well," he said, "it's early yet."

"Guess again," the killer sneered. "It's later than you think."

She felt him tensing, muscles bunching for the move that would ignite the final conflagration. Toni had perhaps an instant to decide upon her strategy and put it into action. Any longer, and she would be trapped between the blazing guns.

Except that Frank LaMancha would not fire, would not defend himself if it involved a risk of harming her. She knew it just as surely as she knew her name—and with the knowledge came a desperate revelation.

It was up to her.

Beyond the throbbing pain inside her twisted arm and shoulder, Toni was aware of other feelings. Pressure. Stress. The rasp of denim jeans against her palm. A subtle swelling underneath the fabric.

Plan and action ran together, merging into one as Toni shifted her position slightly, slid her open hand along his fly and downward, groping blindly for the target. She found it, closed her fingers, put her weight behind the twisting squeeze.

The gunner stiffened, arched his spine as an unearthly scream ripped out of him. The silver pistol wavered off target for an instant, and the tight, restraining arm was gone now, clutching at his injured genitals.

She seized the moment, whipped an arm around and backward, drove the elbow square into his face. Toni felt his glasses buckle, twist, and then the pistol in his fist exploded.

The shock wave deafened her; a tongue of flame licked out to sear her cheek. The lady lost her balance, stumbled, fell. Above her head, the smoky thunder battered back and forth from duelling weapons.

Toni Chadwick hugged the earth and breathed a silent, desperate prayer.

THE SIGHT OF TONI in the gunman's clutches nearly paralyzed Mack Bolan. For an instant, he was gripped by Arctic numbness, piercing to the marrow of his bones. His vision seemed to ripple, and the lady's face was changing, melting swiftly into that of someone else.

Into the face of April Rose.

Bolan saw her in the flickering firelight with a sudden crystal clarity. She was alive and running toward him, arms outstretched and reaching in the heartbeat that remained before a heavy bullet ripped beloved flesh. Her dying scream reverberated in the echo chamber of his mind.

And instantly, the soldier was returned to here and now, transported back from painful past to brutal present. It was Toni Chadwick standing there in front of him, and Bolan had a chance, however slim, to do it right this time.

Another moment left, at most, and Bolan knew that he could make the shot, no sweat. Just swing the Colt Commander up and into target acquisition, let the mercenary's lag time do the rest.

Except for Toni.

He could not squeeze off in rapid fire without a risk of hitting her, and there was no damn time to aim. No cover close enough to reach before his adversary opened fire.

Bolan saw the lady's move before she made it, revealed in her eyes and posture. When the gunman started screaming, Toni broke away and whipped an elbow blindly backward, hammering his face. The mirrored glasses buckled, broke, and Bolan glimpsed a flash of blood from flattened nostrils as she fell away.

He swung the Colt Commander up, already squeezing off as his assailant's .44 exploded aimlessly. The gunner staggered, lurching to his left, and Bolan's bullet took him in the shoulder, spinning the guy around and dumping him in the dust.

Incredibly, the automatic's slide locked open on the smoking, empty chamber. Whether the Commander's owner had already used the other rounds, or had unaccountably forgotten to load the weapon to capacity, no time remained to mull the varied possibilities.

The captured gun was empty, useless, and the wounded pistolero was already moving, wriggling on his side toward the fallen Smith & Wesson.

Bolan dropped the .45 and rushed the Cowboy, sprinting flat out in a race with Death. And he was running second best until he launched himself head-long across the final stretch of ground, impacting belly-down across his adversary's shoulders.

Something tore beneath his arm, and underneath the sudden pain, he felt a spurt of blood, announcing the disintegration of his final sutures.

The force of Bolan's touchdown left him breathless. Beneath his weight, the Cowboy wriggled, twisted, snarling like a wounded animal. With desperate, heaving motions he was trying to dislodge the burden that held him down. His scrabbling hands were inches from the stainless Magnum hand cannon.

Bolan tangled fingers in the Cowboy's hair and twisted, wrenching the enemy's skull over to one side. His free hand locked around a wrist and pinned the crawling hand to earth.

That left the gunman with a single arm at liberty, and he was using it with swift precision, hammering the elbow into Bolan's wounded side. The blows were jarring him, each impact driving bolts of agony through Bolan's abdomen. A bloody, surging darkness threatened to envelop him, and Bolan's grip was slackening involuntarily. The warrior closed his eyes, and jagged streaks of lightning danced across the inside of his eyelids.

Bolan dragged the gunner's head back, twisting with his weight behind the move. In a single fluid motion, he released the captive wrist and whipped his arm around the Cowboy's straining throat, closing the vise in an instant. Frantically, he dug the earth with feet and knees, rolling over onto his back and dragging the Cowboy along with him. They finished the roll with Bolan on his back and the mercenary stretched out, wriggling on top of him.

The guy was thrashing with his feet and elbows like a capsized tortoise now, and instantly aware of his own desperate peril. Bolan's arm was closing his larynx, choking off his breath, and as the mercenary's head began to swim from lack of oxygen, his throes became more violent, desperate.

Beneath him, Bolan held his grip and tightened it methodically. The gunner's boot heels were slashing at Bolan's shins and ankles. Both hands were up and scrabbling at the jungle fighter's face, but Bolan turned his head away and clamped his eyelids tightly shut against the groping fingers. Bolan made his mind a blank against the pain and focused on the imminence of Death. For one or both of them.

And gradually, the gunner's struggles slackened, finally ceased. In place of violent thrashing, tremors gripped his lanky form, a spastic trembling that was beyond control. He stiffened, shuddered out of it, stiffened once again—and finally he was still.

Bolan held his grip another moment, finally loosening his stranglehold by slight degrees. When there was no renewed resistance, Bolan pushed the man's dead weight away and wriggled out from under him. He found the Smith & Wesson .44 instinctively, and it was in his hand, the hammer back and ready, when he made it to his knees.

The fallen mercenary lay on his side, facing Bolan. Glassy eyes and blotchy, mottled cheeks, the dark, protruding tongue—his face bore all the classic signs of strangulation. Bolan knew that he was dead as hell—and still the warrior could not let it go.

The .44 was heavy, dragging down his arm until he braced it with both his hands and brought it onto target acquisition. A fire was singing in his veins, invigorating him, compelling him to action. And the Executioner was smiling when he squeezed the trigger.

22

Sheriff Bobby Heenan lit a cigarette in hopes that it would overpower the antiseptic smell that came with hospitals and doctors. It helped a little, and he took another drag before addressing himself to the figure in the bed before him.

"You were lucky, Jase. Six inches either way, and I'd be talking to your widow now."

Jason Chadwick tried to smile around his pain and medication.

"Too bad you had to make the drive for nothing."

"I was in the neighborhood. Besides, from what I saw around your place, it's good to meet a genuine survivor."

Jason frowned.

"The votes aren't in on that yet."

"You wouldn't want to make a liar out of old Doc Carver, would you?"

Silence fell between them for a moment and extended to embarrassing dimensions. Each man seemed to read the other's mind, his mood, and neither wanted to address the questions that divided them. In the end, Bobby Heenan's badge and temperament compelled him to break the ice.

"I want to get this straight before I tackle my

report," he said. "The way I understand it, these four hoodlums—did I get that right? You did say four?"

"That's right."

"Okay, then. These four hoodlums show up outta nowhere with their guns and their explosives, loaded up for bear, and then they take you hostage in your house for no apparent reason."

Jason eyed him levelly.

"I never said they didn't have a reason. Reckon they just didn't take me into their confidence."

The sheriff nodded.

"Well, that's understandable," he said, "with everything they must've had to think about. I mean, what with wiring up your windows to the wall outlets an' all."

"They seemed to know what they were doing."

Bobby Heenan's smile was closer to a smirk.

"It didn't seem to help them much, now, did it?" He cleared his throat and forged ahead, not waiting for the farmer to reply. "I want to get this straightened out inside my head. You've got these four gorillas in the house, and then here comes a dozen more."

"I wouldn't think a dozen," Jason interjected.

"Well, you'd better think again. I spent my morning counting 'em—or what was left to count. You've got sixteen of 'em piled up like cord wood down at Duffy's funeral home."

The farmer watched him, saying nothing.

"Lemme see, where was I? There you've got these four gorillas in the house, all wired and fortified for doomsday, and then here comes another dozen hot to knock 'em off. They crash your doors and windows, try to come up through the floor and chop their way in through the roof. Before they're done, they've killed each other off across the board. No survivors. That about the size of it?''

The farmer nodded cautiously.

''Jase, you've been shovellin' the shit my way since I came through that door. I know it, and *you* know I know it.''

Jason kept his peace, but he was watching Bobby Heenan closely, thinly veiled suspicion in his eyes.

''I may be a two-bit country sheriff looking at retirement come the next election, but I didn't just fall off the turnip truck this morning. There's no way I can buy that story. Just no way at all.''

''I don't know what to tell you,'' Jason said. His tone was not apologetic in the least.

''Well, you could start by telling me who made the call.''

''What?''

''The call that fetched my deputies to your place,'' Heenan told him patiently. ''Your line was down, the gunsels killed each other off. . . I just keep wonderin' who was it made that call.''

''I couldn't say. A neighbor, maybe.''

''No, I shouldn't think so. A neighbor would've called first sign of trouble. This was almost like somebody *had* to wait before he dropped the dime. Like he was busy.''

''Busy?''

Sheriff Heenan answered with a question of his own.

"You absolutely sure the hoodlums killed each other off? No chance that one or two of them got out alive?"

The farmer risked a grin.

"I can't imagine why they'd send for you."

It was the sheriff's turn to scowl.

"I'll give you that...and knowing you for thirty years the way I have, I know whatever happened out there wasn't your idea."

"All right."

"All right, my ass. I ought to haul you up on charges of obstructing justice and suppressing evidence."

"So, do it."

"Sure. And see it all thrown out for lack of cause. No, thank you."

"Well, then, it looks like you got problems."

"Not at all," the lawman countered. "All those fellows out at Duffy's—they have the problem. Could be you've got trouble, too."

The farmer watched him silently.

"Whoever made that call was part of what went on last night. The time may come when he decides to shut you up for good."

And Jason smiled at that. For just a second there, Bobby Heenan thought the farmer was about to laugh at him.

"I'll take my chances."

Heenan nodded.

"Fair enough. You have a change of heart, I'm in the book." He hesitated at the doorway, turning back toward Jason. "You're on your own."

"G'bye, Bobby."

A HUNDRED MILES AWAY and pushing south behind the wheel of Jason Chadwick's pickup truck, Mack Bolan faced the morning sunlight with cautious optimism. The wound beneath his arm was clean and stitched by Toni's caring hands; the borrowed clothing, torn and bloodied in his final fight for life, had been replaced by spotless cotton shirt and jeans. A shopping bag beside him on the seat contained provisions; underneath the seat, a captured pistol and an Uzi submachine gun nestled in concealment, primed and ready to take on all comers.

He was clean and fed, refreshed, but Bolan's momentary optimism reached beyond the physical. As always, he was moving out of danger into danger, leaving death and ruin in his wake, but there was something riding with him that renewed the Executioner and made him feel rejuvenated.

He had encountered something at the Chadwick farm, amid the killing and the carnage, that reminded him of why he fought his lonely, everlasting war. The warmth and caring he had found with Toni, certainly. . . and something else.

An inner strength, damn right.

The kind of tempered steel inside of living, breathing human beings that revealed itself in desperate times.

A shining light that was uncovered only in the darkest hours of the human soul.

Bolan knew the flame, sure. It had been guiding him along the hellfire trail throughout his adult life, and it would carry him another mile or two before he laid the martial burden down forever.

As long as there were others out there like the Chadwicks, Bolan knew he would not have to make the trek alone. The gentle civilizers still remembered how to fight at need; they had the grit and stamina to see the battle through, to wage a ceaseless, brutal battle of attrition with the savages.

The people of America were waking from a generation's slumber, fitfully at first, and never all at once—but they were getting there. They only needed time, and it would be a soldier's task to buy the time required. If necessary, he would make the purchase with his own blood.

Bolan checked the gas gauge, settled back on creaky springs, and put the pedal to the metal, eating up the prairie highway. Off to either side, the morning sun was turning fields of grain to rippling, burnished gold. It was going to be one hell of a beautiful day.

FIRST KILL
From Mack Bolan's journal:

"I stand alone at the edge of creation, as much an observer as a participant."

Those words, written by me so long ago, are the best way to describe my belief in the higher powers that control our destinies. It reminds me of the first time, in Vietnam, I was called upon to kill a man.

Our camp had been taking heavy fire from a Vietcong sniper. Almost a fourth of the men had been hit by the guy. A lot of nerves were frazzled. I was ready when Colonel Crawford ordered me into the jungle on a search-and-destroy mission against the VC hitman. I had managed to gain an understanding of the Vietcong from questioning natives of the area at great length.

The guy was a savage, pure and simple. He had been making hits in the area for several months, each time forcing the villagers to hide him from our patrols. One mother told me that he beheaded her infant son when she refused to cooperate. Yeah, they were ready to hand the guy up to anyone who could help them.

A village elder explained the pattern of the sniper's attacks. While he was a crack shot, he had no imagination. The old-timer was certain the gunman would hit from the east, shooting across the camp toward the officer's quarters. The best vantage point to watch for him was from the south.

I left the camp and headed north. After a two-mile hike I turned and circled around behind the south perimeter of the camp.

I spotted a stand of trees and climbed up the tallest. I had an excellent view. Before I got up there, I discovered that it was one of the drops that the Cong had used. He had left empty shells and other traces. Yeah, the view was perfect. I had the guy at a disadvantage; he would be sighting against the setting sun. I began scanning for the sniper. I found him as the evening sunlight glinted off the lens of his scope. I centered him in the cross hairs of my rifle.

For an instant, I was down there with him. I knew what he thought and I felt what he felt. Even more, I understood him in a way that I would not have thought possible. I also understood the reason for my mission. I squeezed the trigger and saw the look of surprise on his face as the bullet plowed into his skull.

That day I learned how to kill. By the official count, I had executed nearly 90 VC high rankers before I was called home to begin a fight for an even higher power. No, I do not claim to be chosen by God as an instrument of vengeance. I simply have a duty to do.

Robert E. Lee once said that duty is the sublimest word in our language. That a soldier shouldn't try to do more and shouldn't want to do less. Edmund Burke said that the only thing necessary for the triumph of evil is for good men to stand by and do nothing. This says it in a nutshell.

I have an obligation—no, make that a duty. A duty to the innocents of the Universe not to let the savages trample them. I cannot stand by while gentle civilizers are raped, murdered and consumed by Animal Man.

I would never attempt to command Heaven, but Hell I'll

gladly commandeer. Yeah, give me the hellgrounds to walk. There I can do what I was created to do. I know that I am the last line of defense in this struggle between the universal concepts of good and evil.

I walk tall and proud, living large in the hope that when my time comes, I might die large. While I may sometimes regret the course that my life has taken, I know that I would never attempt to change it. I know what I am and who I am. And with each day that passes, whenever I hear of the savageness of the terrormongers, no matter what their pedigree, I, Mack Bolan, The Executioner, know *why* I am.

For every innocent killed by the savages, my soul feels the burden. So, to ease the weight of those innocent souls, I wage war upon the Cannibals.

I deal out death in the name of life. A paradox, sure, but one that gives meaning to life. I kill to preserve the chance for life of the innocent child in Belfast, Beirut, and anywhere that the savages are trying to stop the progression of man to a higher state of both confidence and mind. Savage Man cannot live in a world that he cannot dominate.

Some have called me a savage also. In a way they are right. But, as with all things, there is a difference. I fight the battle for the side of Justice. I bring cleansing fire to the vermin-ridden nests of humanity. I do what I must because I have to. I know that I can make a difference!

My fate is in the hands of the Universe. I am only the instrument, used to help create hope where the Savages have destroyed hope. I fight oppression for those who cannot fight.

Live large, mankind. There is still much to be done.

MORE ADVENTURE NEXT MONTH WITH

MACK BOLAN

#69 Skysweeper

Hostaged mind

Lasers! The word holds a promise for peace in the world. And the U.S. is twenty years ahead of its nearest rival in the use of the device.

But the secret of this technology lies in the tangled psyche of a former POW, brainwashed years before and unleashed on an unsuspecting America. And the Russians hold the key. Mack Bolan is frighteningly familiar with the mind-control techniques used on prisoners in Vietnam.

The specter of that bloody war haunts The Executioner's current mission as a trail of treachery leads him to an attempt on the President's life and a world-threatening plot masterminded by Bolan's deadliest enemy.

Strakhov returns.

Available wherever paperbacks are sold.

ACTION! ADVENTURE! SUSPENSE! ROMANCE!

**Available soon from
Gold Eagle Books**

THE TAKERS

by Jerry Ahern

bestselling author of *The Survivalist*

Josh Culhane, two-fisted adventurer who'll go anywhere, do anything, teams up with the sexy scholar Mary Mulrooney in a breathtaking pursuit of the satanic Steiglitz and his slinky, psychotic daughter.

Culhane and Mulrooney battle halfway across the globe, through all the labyrinths of human history and myth, to a last stand beneath the Antarctic ice cap, where they find an ancient starbase whose builders had never gotten home!

THE TAKERS is an unbeatable experience. Three hundred and eighty-four pages of spellbinding, page-turning high-adventure reading! Compelling action in the spirit of *Raiders of the Lost Ark*.

Available soon wherever paperbacks are sold.

HE'S EXPLOSIVE. HE'S MACK BOLAN... AGAINST ALL ODDS

He learned his deadly skills in Vietnam...then put them to good use by destroying the Mafia in a blazing one-man war. Now **Mack Bolan** ventures further into the cold to take on his deadliest challenge yet—the KGB's worldwide terror machine.

Follow the lone warrior on his exciting new missions...and get ready for more nonstop action from his high-powered combat teams: **Able Team**—Bolan's famous Death Squad—battling urban savagery too brutal and volatile for regular law enforcement. And **Phoenix Force**—five extraordinary warriors handpicked by Bolan to fight the dirtiest of antiterrorist wars, blazing into even greater danger.

Fight alongside these three courageous forces for freedom in all-new action-packed novels! Travel to the gloomy depths of the cold Atlantic, the scorching sands of the Sahara, and the desolate Russian plains. You'll feel the pressure and excitement building page after page, with nonstop action that keeps you enthralled until the explosive conclusion!

Now you can have all the new Gold Eagle novels delivered right to your home!

You won't want to miss a single one of these exciting new action-adventures. And you don't have to! Just fill out and mail the card at right, and we'll enter your name in the Gold Eagle home subscription plan. You'll then receive six brand-new action-packed Gold Eagle books every other month, delivered right to your home! You'll get two Mack Bolan novels, one Able Team and one Phoenix Force, plus one book each from two thrilling, new Gold Eagle libraries, **SOBs** and **Track**. In **SOBs** you'll meet the legendary team of mercenary warriors who fight for justice and win. **Track** features a military and weapons genius on a mission to stop a maniac whose dream is everybody's worst nightmare. Only Track stands between us and nuclear hell!

FREE! The New War Book and Mack Bolan bumper sticker.

As soon as we receive your card we'll rush you the long-awaited New War Book and Mack Bolan bumper sticker—both ABSOLUTELY FREE. Then under separate cover, you'll receive your six Gold Eagle novels.

The New War Book is *packed* with exciting information for Bolan fans: a revealing look at the hero's life...two new short stories...book character biographies...even a combat catalog describing weapons used in the novels! The New War Book is a special collector's item you'll want to read again and again. And it's yours FREE when you mail your card!

Of course, you're under no obligation to buy anything. Your first six books come on a 10-day free trial—if you're not thrilled with them, just return them and owe nothing. The New War Book and bumper sticker are yours to keep, FREE!

Don't miss a single one of these thrilling novels...mail the card now, while you're thinking about it.

HE'S UNSTOPPABLE.
AND HE'LL FIGHT
TO DEFEND FREEDOM!

Mail this coupon today!

FREE! THE NEW WAR BOOK AND MACK BOLAN BUMPER STICKER
when you join our home subscription plan.

Gold Eagle Reader Service, a division of Worldwide Library
In U.S.A.: 2504 W. Southern Avenue, Tempe, Arizona 85282
In Canada: P.O. Box 2800, Postal Station 'A', 5170 Yonge Street,
Willowdale, Ont. M2N 5T5

YES, rush me The New War Book and Mack Bolan bumper sticker FREE, and, under separate cover, my first six Gold Eagle novels. These first six books are mine to examine free for 10 days. If I am not entirely satisfied with these books, I will return them within 10 days and owe nothing. If I decide to keep these novels, I will pay just $1.95 per book (total $11.70). I will then receive the six Gold Eagle novels every other month, and will be billed the same low price of $11.70 per shipment. I understand that each shipment will contain two Mack Bolan novels, and one each from the Able Team, Phoenix Force, SOBs and Track libraries. There are no shipping and handling or any other hidden charges. I may cancel this arrangement at any time, and The New War Book and bumper sticker are mine to keep as gifts, even if I do not buy any additional books.

166-BPM-PADZ

Name	(please print)	
Address		Apt. No.
City	State /Province	Zip/Postal Code
Signature	(If under 18, parent or guardian must sign.)	

This offer limited to one order per household. We reserve the right to exercise discretion in granting membership. Offer expires December 31, 1984

MB-SUB-3×